MENDED HEARTS

LISAMARIE KADE

KADE PUBLISHING LLC

This book is a work of fiction. Names, characters, places, and incidents either are products of the author's imagination or are used fictitiously. Any resemblance to actual events or locals or persons, living or dead, is coincidental.

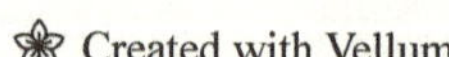 Created with Vellum

This book is dedicated to those that believe in second chances.

PROLOGUE

Ashton
9 years old

I was out running through the fields, letting my tears fall freely. My mama was gone and according to her letter, she wasn't planning on coming back. Daddy was sitting at the kitchen table with an unreadable expression. Like me, he too had a letter from Mama. If I had to guess, it was similar to mine. She done left us to fend for ourselves. Why didn't she want me? It was the last thing I asked Aunt Lynne before she shooed me out the back door. She never did answer me.

I ran until the tears stung and blurred my vision. I finally collapsed in the apple orchard next to our property. I lay there between the trees and let my sobs take over.

"Hey, girl, what's your problem?"

Was someone talking to me? I tried to control my breathing and listened. I heard nothing. Just when I thought I was hearing things, that voice called out again.

"Did you hear me?" a boy asked as he stepped out from behind a tree.

I stared back in what could only be described as disbelief. I ran this field all the time and I ain't never seen no one except the workers before.

"Don't you talk?" he asked, and I don't know why but it made me mad.

"Didn't your mama teach you manners?" I quipped back. Boy, was he rude.

"The same question can be asked to you."

My mama. I burst into tears at the thought of her. I covered my face with my hands and hoped for the boy to go away.

Not even a minute later, that rude boy was pulling my hands from my face. What does he think he is doing?

"Hey, don't cry."

"Go away," I snapped.

"You're on my farm so I'm not going anywhere."

That got my attention. His farm? What does he mean by that?

"What do you mean *your farm*?"

"Just what I said. This was my granddad's farm and now it's ours."

"Oh."

"What's wrong with you?"

"Nothing." I wasn't about to tell this boy my problems. I didn't even know his name.

"Alright then, I'll leave you to it." The boy let go of my hands and stood to leave.

"Wait, what's your name?" I don't know why, but for some reason I wanted to know his name. I looked up at his blue eyes. They sure were pretty.

He gave me a crooked smile. "Name's Clay, Clay Williams." He nodded his head once and walked off without looking back.

If only I knew back then that Clay would have become so important to me, I might not have let him walk off that day we first met just so I could have known him longer.

1

Ashton
Present day

I feel relieved that I found Brody the perfect gift for our anniversary. I may have found myself a few things too.

As the associate rings me up, I can't help but feel excited. I can't wait to get home, wrap his gift, and slip into some lingerie and wait for him to arrive home. Our two-year anniversary is coming up and things haven't been the best between us, especially in the bedroom. I plan to change that though.

However, when I swipe my card and it is declined not once, but three times, I realize not all is well in the Clark's marriage. I ask the associate, a pretty young woman with brown, shoulder length hair, to put my stuff to the side while I walk outside to call the bank. Surely there is some mistake.

Twenty minutes later and after going through what felt like fifty security questions, I am told that Mr. Clark closed our joint bank account hours earlier. What the fuck?

I call my husband; of course I get his voicemail. Figures.

I don't even have the courage to go back into the department store. I just get in my car and leave.

I can't quite understand why Brody would make such a drastic move and not tell me. Anger is beginning to fester inside of me. I'm not an angry person either, but this has me hot.

To my surprise, Brody's Infinity is parked in the driveway. He's never home this early. In fact, he hasn't been home before eight pm in more than six months. The thought sends chills down my spine, and I can feel the hair on the back of my neck stand.

An uneasy feeling starts to settle in the pit of my stomach as I open the car door to get out. It's actually overriding the anger I was feeling moments prior. The Florida heat smacks me in the face. It's suffocating and suddenly I miss the weather in Nebo. I shake my head as I make my way to the door.

Walking into the house, I notice bags by the entry way. What on earth?

"Brody?"

Silence. I make my way down the hall to our bedroom and peek my head in. When I don't find him there, I make my way back toward the front of the house. An eerie feeling begins to form in the pit of my stomach. He must be in his office. Has to be.

Sure enough, he's in there. I can hear papers being shuffled around. I walk straight in without knocking. Brody hates that, yet I find myself not giving a shit considering he closed our bank accounts without even discussing with me.

"Brody? What's going on?"

He looks like a deer in headlights, like he's actually shocked to see me.

"Ashton… you're home early?" He looks at his watch.

"Yeah, well, when my debit card declines and I can't reach my husband, I have no choice but to come home."

Brody throws his head back, causing his blonde hair to shift. He groans and runs his hands down his face. I know he's not the one annoyed right now. I have a reason to be, but not him.

He finally looks back to me and sits at his desk.

"Ashton, we need to talk."

"So talk." My hands are on my hips now, and I'm growing more pissed with each minute that passes.

"Um, well… there's no easy way to say this. I closed the account because…"

There's a pause as he grabs the back of his neck. He looks stressed out and for a brief moment, I begin to worry that something is seriously wrong.

I raise my eyebrows at him. "Because why, Brody?"

"Because… I'm moving out and want a divorce."

"Wha… what?" I am taken aback. A divorce? Moving out? This is a joke right?

"Ashton, look, you and me... we are different people."

"What the hell does that mean?" I bark. This man better start spilling it before I lose it.

"Come on. We haven't really been into each other for a while now. Some days I think you're stuck in your past, and I am realizing I'm not really ready to settle down."

Of course he brings up my past. It's something that has come up several times since we've been together. But his statement about not being ready to settle down throws me for a loop.

"Are you… have you cheated on me?" I can barely get the words out. They taste bitter to even speak.

"What?! No I haven't, though I have flirted with other women and have had conversations with them. It's what has made me realize I don't want to settle down."

It's as if the wind has been knocked out of me. I take a step back. Here I am planning our anniversary, trying to make this work, and he's been planning to leave me.

"You can't just close the bank account. We're married and it's *our* money." I bust my ass and I'm not about to let him just take it all. Who does he think he is?

"Well, I did. I can't have you draining me." Brody says it like he's annoyed. He can't be serious. I've never been some gold digger. I work and I help pay the bills.

"That money is just as much mine as it is yours," I state loudly, as anger starts to overtake the blow that Brody just dropped at my feet. Maybe it's the other way around. I can't be sure; too many emotions are running through me as I try to process everything.

Brody pays me no attention as he opens his desk drawer and pulls out an envelope.

"This is for you." He walks around his desk with the envelope still in his hand and hands it to me.

I snatch it from him; it's not sealed and there's money in it. My eyes fly back up to his.

"Calm down, Ashton, it's just until we get things sorted and a judge decides." He walks past me and out of his office.

Why is he so unaffected? It's as if he isn't in love with me and hasn't been for quite a while.

I turn around to follow him. Why? I don't even know at this point. I'm livid and in shock.

"Where are you going?" Yep, I'm stupid enough to ask, yet a part of me cares to know. He is my husband, well, was.

"I'm going to my new place. You can keep this place."

I stop dead in my tracks. The reality of what he just said hits me in the face. He's already got a new place to live. I will be living here alone. Alone in a big town house that we rent in a prime location, I might add.

"Wow," I barely manage to whisper, more so to myself than him. I feel the threat of tears, and it takes everything in me to keep them at bay. He doesn't deserve to see my sadness. I refuse to crumble in front of him.

Brody gathers up the bags that sit in the entry way. They make sense now. He looks back to me one last time and gives me a sad smile. That's it. Nothing else is said as he turns and walks out of our home.

Did all that really just happen? How can this be happening to me? How can I have not known he has been planning this? I ask myself a million questions. Questions that will most likely never be answered. I'm astonished that Brody pulled the rug out from under me. Without me even knowing. Was I that blind to not see our relationship crumbling? No, I loved him and I thought he loved me back. I walk in a daze to the kitchen and pour myself a glass of wine. I finish it almost immediately and pour another. I can feel the anger slowly fading away. I want to be angry, yet I shouldn't be. Closing my eyes, I allow my mind to wonder back over the last few years.

2

Ashton

I met Brody at a college party. One I didn't even want to attend but Anna, the girl I shared a dorm with, insisted I live a little. Brody and I didn't hit it off right away; he came on way too strong and I wasn't looking for a one night stand. In fact, I wasn't really looking for anything.

Brody finally gave up on trying to get in my pants and we eventually had a fun conversation. From there we started to spend a lot of time together and I finally caved, hoping it would put an end to all things Clay. Getting him out of my mind and my heart, I slept with Brody. It didn't help much but I welcomed the distraction.

One wild and crazy night he asked me to marry him and I shook my head yes without even thinking twice. Now looking back, I realize how stupid that was. I think in my young, warped mind, I thought that if I married Brody Clark, the gorgeous frat boy with blonde hair and brown eyes, that I would forget all about the hole in my heart. That I would forget all about Clay Williams, the boy I left behind so he could chase his dreams. Deep down I knew I still loved Clay. Don't get me wrong, I loved Brody, but our love was different. It wasn't deep. Sure, we enjoyed being around each other and he made me happy. Even though I knew there was something missing, I let this relationship continue. I decide another glass of wine is needed.

Once married, we settled into a routine. He was finished with college and excelling in his career. He worked business management at one of the casinos nearby. I didn't mind the long hours or the time he spent away. I threw myself into the world of fashion. I had my Bachelors in fashion merchandising and was working hard to prove my worth in the oh so very competitive market.

I'd always loved fashion, but growing up in a small town left little to choose from when it came to shopping. When I decided to leave Nebo, I made sure I was going to a college where I could study fashion. It's the one thing I don't regret doing while looking back at the mess I've created. I know now that I married Brody for the wrong reasons. Now to figure out how to clean the mess up and move on.

I should call Sunny and my aunt, but I'm not ready to face them… to hear the *I told you so* remarks. Sunny doesn't like Brody, not one bit. As for Aunt Lynne, well, she damn sure doesn't like him. She says he isn't a country boy and is too full of himself. She has stated more than once that he doesn't know how to take care of a woman properly. She isn't wrong. Brody is arrogant and all about himself. Maybe that's what drew me to him; he didn't send a lot of time on me. He was always too busy with himself. *Ugh...* the writing was written on the wall and I chose not to look at it.

I get up to pour myself more wine and realize I finished the bottle. On. My. Own. That's when the first tears begin to fall. *Oh well*, I think to myself as I pull another bottle of sweet red off of the wine rack. The hurt will come tomorrow, but for tonight I will forget.

———

After nursing my headache and showering, I decide that I need to sit down and figure out my new reality. I have so much to figure out. Who is keeping what? How much will I have in bills on my own? There is just so much that comes with a divorce.

After an hour of making notes and leaving a few messages for attorneys to call me back. I decide to swallow my pride and call my best friend.

After two rings she picks up.

"Hey, Ash, what's up?"

Sunny is one of the few people I still allow to call me by my nickname. When I left home and my past behind, I no longer let anyone call me Ash. It was a painful reminder of all I left and I just couldn't handle it. Anyone new I meet in Florida call me Ashton and if one of them slips and calls me Ash for short, I set them in their place quick. Anna and my other friends learned quickly.

I take a breath. "So much is suddenly up, well, down really."

"Oh no, what's happened?"

"I came home yesterday to Brody asking for a divorce."

I sigh and wait for the lecture that is sure to come. Sunny has only met Brody two times. Neither time went over well. She was pissed when I ran off and married him without telling her. She got over it, of course, but it took a solid six months or so before she started to get over it.

"Shut the front door! Hallelujah! This is the best news I've heard since… well, forever."

"Gee, thanks."

"Just tellin' ya like it is." I hear her sigh. "So what are you gonna do now?"

"I'm not sure yet. I need to sit down with a lawyer, I guess, and figure it all out." I take a deep breath. This is overwhelming. It suddenly occurs to me that I haven't cried since last night while downing all the wine.

"Earth to Ashton… Are ya there?" Sunny's southern accent brings me back to present.

"Sorry, I got lost in thought. What did you say?"

"I reckon you are stuck in your head. Always have been." Sunny pauses before continuing on, "I asked if you wanted me to come down and help you with things."

"Oh." I wasn't expecting that. "That's not necessary, I'm sure I'll be able to get this mess sorted out. We don't have a lot invested in each other."

That is the truth. We have no children together. I own my small SUV and his car is in his name only. The only thing we share together is our townhouse and up until yesterday, our bank account. The rest of the details are really minor, like furniture and all that. I just want to make sure he isn't running off with money that I have earned, that's my main concern.

"Ya know you can always come back home. Nebo can use some fashion."

I laugh and then cringe at the thought of going home.

My fashion tastes will cause the old ladies to have heart attacks. They'll never approve of such bold and unique styles.

I cringe because the thought of actually going home causes an ache in my chest and it terrifies me. I left a lot of people angry.

"No way would Nebo want me these days, Sunny. I'm sure I'll get along just fine after the shock wears off."

Well. Alright then, but. Ash…"

I know what's coming. She's going to tell me to call Aunt Lynne.

"It's time to call your aunt. "

I called it. Some things never change.

"I will. She's next up on my list."

"Love ya, girl. Call me anytime."

"Love ya back."

We end the call and I stare at my phone. I don't want to call my aunt. I mean, I do because, well, I love her, but calling her always causes me stress and I have enough of that. I contemplate calling her tomorrow, but if I know Sunny, she'll tell her by sundown, so I better get to it.

3

Ashton

When I dial Aunt Lynne, part of me hopes that she
doesn't answer, that she'll be busy at the bakery,
making apple something for the locals.

My aunt owns Lynne's Bakery. It is the only bakery in
town. She purchases fresh apples weekly from you guessed it,
Clay's family. I run a hand over my face, hoping each ring is
the last before her voicemail kicks in.

No such luck as my aunt finally picks up.

"Hello?"

"Hey, Aunt Lynne"

"Ashton dear, how are you? How's Florida treatin' you?"

I sigh. "I've been better, but Florida is fine."

"You've been better?"

It's a question, a loaded one at that.

"Yes, things are a tad difficult at the moment."

I stall because I'm a chicken shit. There I said it. I was too chicken to face Clay so I ran, ran straight into Brody at stupidville, and now look at me.

"Well, Ashton, you gonna spill it? I ain't got a lot of time. Apple pies are about ready to come out of the oven."

"Yes, sorry." Here goes nothing. "Brody asked for a divorce."

I wait and brace myself for her response.

"I see. I imagine that's a difficult predicament to be in."

"A bit."

I don't know what else to say, yet I know she has more she wants to say so I wait a bit more.

My aunt clears her throat and I know it's coming.

"Well… dear, I knew eventually this day would come. It's for the best, Ashton. The sooner you see that, the better. Just think, now you can come back home and start living again.

"I am living," I say bleakly as I run my hands through my hair. She always brings up coming home.

"Nonsense, dear, you are just existing. Aside from your career, you are not living to your full potential and I think it's time you get to it."

"I'll get along just fine. As soon as the dust settles, I'll be good. I promise."

"Honey, you ain't fine. Since the day you hightailed it out of here, you became a ghost of who you were. Now that Brody wasn't the man for you. He sure ain't nothin' to cry over either. He didn't love you the way you need to be loved. I bet if you come on back, Clay would love…"

"Aunt Lynne!" I interrupt promptly. "No, I'm not coming home, and I sure as heck ain't looking for love. I'm fine. Honestly."

I'm annoyed. I knew she would bring up coming home and Clay. I move to sit the kitchen table and drop my head down on the table.

"Oh, Ashton, my stubborn girl, if you insist, I'll drop it, but only because my pies are done and I gotta get to 'em."

"Alright, I'll call you soon. I love you." I end the call. I'm beyond exhausted, yet glad that call is over.

Come home, my ass. I'd be run out of town so fast, my aunt couldn't blink. My only friend there is Sunny. Everyone else learned to hate me long ago and I have accepted that.

It's all I think about while I go around the house Brody and I shared taking down the photos we had hung in various places. After I gather them all up, I take them straight to the outside trash. No need to save or pack up.

After all, I'm used to throwing things away.

4

Clay
Present day

The smell of warm apple pie hits my nostrils as I enter Lynne's bakery. Lynne had called in another crate of apples even though I had several dropped off yesterday. She requested I do the delivery and that tells me she is up to something.

"Hey, Lynne," I holler; she must be in the back tending to one of her creations.

"Be right out."

I take a seat at one of the few tables she has in this place. It's a small shop, but it's always worked. Pale yellow paint on the walls with red accents throughout it. This little place screams southern, always has, always will.

Lynne comes out and catches me scrubbing my face.

"Why, Clay, what's got you looking down?"

I smile and tell her nothing and that I am fine. This woman

already knows. Being in this bakery brings back a flood of memories. The scent of apples will forever be burned in my memory as h*er scent.* Yeah, I know I own an apple farm, but I don't do apple pies or any apple baked goods. Not since she left.

I shake the thoughts of her and focus.

"I have your crate; where would you like me to put it?"

The sooner I get this task done, the sooner I can get out of the bakery and breathe without feeling like I'm suffocating.

"Right back here will be fine." Lynne gestures to a spot behind the counter.

I have to keep my eyes focused on the crate and not look at the counter, behind the counter… hell, this whole place makes my chest ache. I picture her everywhere in here. Even after all these years. I take a deep breath. Fuck her. She left me.

I set the crate down and look back to Lynne. She's watching me carefully. I don't like it. I hope my face doesn't give me away, getting lost in memories of Ashton, the niece she helped raise.

"My dear boy, let me make you something to drink. Go sit." She waves me off toward the front.

I want to argue that I have work to be getting back to, except it's Lynne. There's no arguing with that woman. She's always be independent and strong willed. It's where Ashton got it from. Reluctantly, I take a seat again and remove my cowboy hat.

Less than a minute later, Lynne walks out with a sweet ice tea and a piece of apple pie that she knows damn well I won't touch. I don't know why she bothers.

"Here ya are, Clay. It's on the house."

"Thank you, ma'am." I nod and take a sip of my drink.

"Ashton called today."

Of course she did. That's probably why I have been called

down here. I should have known that's why she called me down here. I should have sent Blue down. He would enjoy this apple shit and Lynne's never ending life advice. But nope, here I sit, about to endure it with a smile on my face.

When I don't respond to Lynne, she takes it as her cue to continue.

"She's getting a divorce."

She's what?! I nearly spit my tea out. Instead I swallow and start coughing. Lynne comes over and pats me on the back.

"I know, such wonderful news. I hope she moves back home where she belongs. Ya know?"

"That's a shame to hear her marriage didn't work out. I doubt she'll be moving back though, Lynne."

Ashton come back? After she took off in the middle of the night? Not a chance in hell she'd come back. I feel a rush of anger trying to break through the walls I sealed off long ago. I take a deep breath. I'm not sure what she is expecting me to say. What I want to say is, I don't give a rat's ass about Ashton and her failed marriage. Karma got her ass and I have no sympathy for her. I don't say this out loud. If I did, Lynne would surely slap my face and tell me to mind my manners.

"It's no shame, boy. I'm glad she's getting a divorce. That Brody ain't good enough for her, but I know someone who is."

So Brody is his name. I had heard she got married, but never heard his name around town. Lynne and Sunny made sure they never spoke about it in front of me, not until today anyway.

Lynne pulls the seat out in front of me and sits down, not a good sign. I know where this is headed and I don't like it. I need to bail out and fast.

"Well, I suppose I better get back to it." I toss my thumb over my shoulder toward to door, hoping she'll take the hint to drop this, whatever it is.

"You haven't touched your pie yet. Eat up; you can't be running on empty, especially in this heat."

She's not wrong about the heat. It's warmer than usual for this time of year. It's the end of May and it's already hitting 80 degrees. I force myself to pick up the fork, stab the damn pie that I don't want, and shove it in my mouth. All while cringing. I hate fucking apple pie. Because of Ashton Carpenter, I'll never enjoy it again.

"Maybe if you reach out to Ashton, you can get her to come home."

Lynne's words cause me to choke on the damn pie. I cough several times and have to take a drink just to clear my throat. She can't be serious. I look up and make eye contact with her. She smiles and wiggles her eyebrows at me. Yup, she's damn serious. I can't do this. Time to squash whatever hopes Lynne has.

I clear my throat again. "No, ma'am, that's not a good idea, nor is it gonna happen. Ashton left here without a care, and she's no longer mine to worry about."

My words are clipped and I feel a little bad for that last bit, but it's the truth. I slide my chair back. I'm done here. Grabbing my hat off the table, I put it back on while avoiding eye contact with this stubborn woman.

"But Clay," Lynne stands up along with me. It makes me feel guilty for snapping, yet I refuse to entertain this subject.

"I really got to get back to it. It was great to see you and thank you for tea and pie." I tip my hat and turn and walk away as fast as my legs will move.

I head straight for my pickup. I don't even look back. Lynne could be following me and I'd never know it, that's how angry I have become.

Everyone in this town knows better than to mention Ashton to me. As far as I am concerned, she is dead in my book. I don't want to hear about her marriage, divorce, or any damn thing that involves her. It still makes me so angry. Even after all this time. I hit the steering wheel in frustration.

I decide not to return to the farm. I call Blue and tell him to handle the rest of the day. I am headed to the bar. I need a drink.

5

Clay

I pull into The Neon Moon and walk straight to the bar that is just a few feet away from the entrance. The bar is empty; then again it is only 2:30 in the afternoon. The black walls covered with various posters of country artists welcome me in.

I sit down and waited for Bo to come out from the back. Bo owns the place, took it over from old man Clint. He was due to retire and Bo was looking for something to keep himself out of trouble. It worked out nicely.

"Hey, man, what brings you in this early?" Bo shoots me a questioning look.

"I had a delivery at Lynne's."

"Say no more." Bo turns and pulls down his top shelf whiskey. He knows what I want. I don't need to ask. He slides me the drink. I don't even think, I just down the contents quickly and slide the glass back to him.

He pours another and passes it back. "Wanna talk about it?"

"Ashton is getting a divorce." I pause to down my shot. "Lynne wants me to talk Ashton into moving back home."

"Shit, man, that's a load dropped at your feet. What did you say?" Bo pulls up a stool he keeps behind the counter for slow days and sits down. He pours another shot for me.

"I told her I ain't the man for the job. This ship has sailed."

I'd like to believe my ship has sailed. Truth be told, I haven't settled down with no woman since her. It's all just sex with no strings attached. I run my hands through my hair. I don't know why I am allowing this to get under my skin.

"Good for you, but seeing how you are up in here, how are you really doing?" Bo asks, worry written all over his face. We never discuss Ashton, even though he lost her too. They were close friends once upon a time.

I pound the shot, knowing it won't be long before the alcohol kicks in. I shake my head. "I don't know, man. I thought I was past all this anger, but just the mention of her name has me seein' red."

"That's probably because you still love her."

My eyes snap up to Bo. "Like hell I do."

He puts his hands up. "Now don't shoot the messenger, but I see it, hell Clay, the whole town of Nebo sees it. Why do you think we tip toe around you when it comes to her? We never mention her." He does the stupid air quote with his hand when he says her.

He's got a point there, no one talks about her to me. No one mentions any memories or past times we've had in this little town. I don't love her though, I can't. Not after what she did to me.

"You should probably try to get laid."

I nod my head to Bo. That's exactly what I need. I'll fuck all thoughts of the girl who broke my heart and crushed our dreams out of my system.

After a while, locals started to mingle in to get their drink on. I'm sure they look at me with pity. I don't care though. Let them think I'm heartbroken. It usually attracts a lonely woman looking for a good time. I can do a good time.

Not even ten minutes later, a brunette wonders up to me like clockwork and asks what I'm drinking.

"Straight whiskey," I reply without looking at her. I know what she's doing. It's what they all do.

From the corner of my eye, I watch her wave Bo over and order a gin and tonic for her and whiskey for me.

"Here ya go, cowboy."

The glass of whiskey is set in front of me and I pause before taking it. I don't love Ashton; it's quite the opposite. I take the shot and slam the tumbler down on the counter. I fucking hate Ashton.

"Wanna get out of here?" I ask.

I look over at the woman and take her in for the first time. She has brown eyes and shiny brown hair that falls just below her shoulders. As I let my eyes wonder down, I notice her tits. They are popping out of her tank top and clearly fake, but I don't give a damn. She's skinny and while I like them with a little meat, Brunette here will do. She will be the distraction I need tonight.

"Hell yeah, I do," she replies, a little too eagerly. I'll be sure to lay down to rules once we get to where we are going.

"Let's go." I stand and realize I might have had a bit too much to drink. I smile at her, hoping she's sober.

She giggles before grabbing me by the hand and pulling me along. "I've only just got here and had one drink, you didn't even let me finish it." She winks as Bo hollers for me to call him later and I wave. He knows this routine. I find a woman, fuck her, and leave her with the I don't do relationships line. Shitty, I know, but that's the reality. I don't sugar coat.

I have her drive about a mile down the road to my other property. I only come to this house occasionally. On the nights I can't bear to think of Ashton and the what could have beens. When the breeze blows a certain way and the scent from the field fills the house, I come here. It's also the only place I bring women back to. I've never taken them to the farm house. Never will.

The fields at the farm house remind me of Ashton and her carefree ways. Closing my eyes, I can picture her running through them. We spent countless hours in them, and what started off as friends grew to a relationship. She was my first love, and damn her if she didn't destroy my heart when she left. I'd be lying if the thoughts don't make me sad and I hate that she still has this hold over me, but I can't seem to shake her memory. Because of Ashton I am a man of stone now.

I point to the street ahead and tell brunette to turn right. She does as she's told without any questions. I like that, it means she's only here for a good time and nothing more. I trace a finger up her thigh to the bottom of her very short shorts; it gives her goose bumps. She glances at me and winks before throwing her dark hair over her shoulder. Another perk, she looks nothing like Ashton. I'm going to enjoy getting lost in her.

We exit her car and she pounces on me right away, leaving all thoughts of Ashton behind.

6

Ashton

A week has gone by since Brody dropped the big D on me —and I don't mean dick. The shock has worn off. I only cried the first night over it. Now I'm sitting here crying over the reality of it.

I can't afford this place on my own.

After going over my expenses and bills, there's no way I can stay in this townhouse alone.

I thought about finding a roommate, but that kind of creeps me out. That's what happens when you live in South Florida, I guess. I really don't have the time to search for a decent and trustworthy roommate.

I met with the attorney I hired, Glenda Moore. She's a tough cookie as my aunt Lynne would say. I don't want any drama really. I just want what I am rightfully owed. I had put some of my money into his projects with the promise he would pay me back. I just want my portion back.

I sigh and look over the documents again. I have loads of student loans to pay off on top of all this.

When I went into my fashion studies, I knew it wouldn't be a cheap deal. I also decided to minor in culinary arts. I had always loved baking with my aunt. I missed that so much when I left home, and taking those courses helped ease the ache in my chest. I, of course, am paying the price now.

There's just no way I can do this alone. I grumble as I shove the papers away.

Calling Sunny for advice will be pointless, but I do it anyhow. When I don't reach her, I leave a voicemail telling her to call me back.

I refuse to call my aunt, not yet.

I decide to make use of my time by packing up more of Brody's things. I'm sure he'll be by sooner or later for them.

———

I finish the bedroom by lunch and head to the kitchen to make lunch. While I'm making a sandwich, my phone rings.

I pick it up to see Sunny's name on the screen.

"Hey, Sunny,"

"Hi, Ash, sorry I missed your call." Sunny giggles and I can't be certain, but I think I hear a male's voice in the background.

"Who's that?" I ask curiously. Last I knew, she was single and not interested in anyone.

"Oh…um… that's just Bo. Remember him?" She giggles as she says that last bit.

"Of course I remember him. He was one of my friends." I'm slightly annoyed that she would ask if I remembered him, even if I might have deserved it. Truth be told, I cut Bo off too. I refused all his texts and calls. It hurt me to do so. Bo was my childhood friend and I was afraid that if I talked to him, that he would persuade me to come home. I would have caved and I just couldn't risk that. As it was, I avoided Sunny for weeks. She was mad as hell when I finally answered the phone. I had to listen to her chew me out for over thirty minutes. I took the verbal beating she gave me; after all I had earned it. By the end of the conversation she had forgiven me, even without me giving her the details on why I left in the first place.

"So. What's up?" Sunny's voice comes through the line and it brings me out of memory lane.

"I… um… just need to pick your thoughts on something. I need another person's point of view." I swallow, knowing what she will most likely say and worrying what Bo will overhear. He'll probably run back to town and tell anyone who will listen. I should call back later, but I haven't made the best of decisions in the last few years so to hell with it.

"Well, spill it," Sunny says.

"Uh, yeah… I can't afford my place on my own." I blurt the words out so fast and then wait for her response.

"You could get a roommate."

I wasn't expecting that response, not from Sunny.

"I thought about that, but I would need a roommate like yesterday."

"Ash, are you not okay… you know, money wise?"

Damn her. She reads into everything, always has, and I know Bo sure heard that. I cringe as I lay my head on the cold granite counter.

"Not exactly. I had given a small chunk of my savings to Brody to invest in his business venture, which my lawyer is working on getting back."

"What?! How stupid are you? Ugh! Don't answer that, we already know you're dumb."

"Thanks, Sunny, appreciate it." Have I mentioned how right she is lately? I sure am dumb. I never questioned Brody, not once.

"You sure done messed up."

"Yeah, she did," I hear Bo holler out in the background. Asshole.

"I know, Sunny. I know…" It's barely a whisper, but she hears me.

"As long as you know." She pauses. "Well, did you look for a cheaper place? What other options do you have?"

I sigh. "I did. Nothing in this city, or county for that matter, is affordable on a single income."

Which I failed to research before I moved. I was living in a college dorm, I didn't have to think about these things. Then I went from living in a dorm to moving in with Brody. He handled the finances. At first I wrote him a check each month and then we thought it would make more sense to do a joint bank account. What a fool I was.

"Sounds like you need to come home then."

Ah, there it is. I knew it was coming. I shake my head. "I can't… don't wanna."

"What other choice do ya have, Ash?"

"I don't know. I was hoping you had better suggestions."

Sunny laughs. "Look, as your friend, I think you need to stop being dumb and stubborn. Just come on home."

I shake my head again as the first tear threatens to fall. "Everyone hates me there. What about my career?"

"Who cares what everyone thinks of ya? Besides, what career will you have if you are homeless living out of your car?"

Ugh, she's right about that second part. I hate that she's right. A thought suddenly comes to my mind.

"Hey, you can always move here."

Sunny snorts and then starts laughing sarcastically.

"I'm serious, Sunny." It's farfetched; however, I'm dead serious.

"I'm not leaving Nebo. I happen to be doing just fine here. Try coming home, you might just do okay too.

"I don't know. I have a few weeks, maybe I'll find a roommate."

I hear talking in the background again. I assume it's still Bo until I hear Sunny speak.

"Hi, Clay." Her words boom through the phone.

Clay. My heart rate picks up a notch.

"Oh, nothing much, just chatting with Ash." No she didn't. She flat out told him she was talking to me. I need to end this call before things get any worse.

"Sunny I need to-" I stop short when I hear his voice.

"What are you doing talkin' to her for? She left you too, or did you forget?"

My mouth drops open at the venom laced words Clay just said. True or not, they fucking stung like a slap to the face. I have to end this call and quick.

But before I can, Sunny is shouting, "Clay Williams! You best hush! Besides, Ash might be coming home."

I want to crawl in a hole, a very dark hole. Here she is telling people my business, people that hate me.

"Sunny!" I yell into the phone. "I gotta go."

I don't even wait for a response. I just hang up and slowly slide down to the floor.

Clay hates me. He hates me for leaving him and clearly he is still angry about it seven years later. Just knowing how mad he is makes me not want to have to move home.

7

Clay

I know I shouldn't have said that to Sunny. I shouldn't have stooped so low, but in the heat of the moment, I didn't care. I wanted to make sure Ashton knew she wasn't welcomed back in Nebo. I said it loud enough; no doubt she heard me, loud and clear.

The look Sunny shot me said I'd hear about that lash out when she ended the call. I'd stay around for the lecture too, lord knows I deserved it and unlike Ashton, I would stick around and not tuck tail and run.

"Ash… you still there? Hello?"

I watch with amusement as Sunny holds the phone out and looks at it. I'd bet a hundred bucks that good ol' Ashton hung up. Sunny looks from the phone cell phone in her hand and then to me. Yup, she hung up.

"Damn you, Clay Williams! Look what you done did. Ash hung up on me." She glares at me with her hands on her hips.

A smile plays on my lips as I shrug my shoulders; better to keep my mouth shut and just let her get on with it.

"Come on now, she might be comin' home and you can't be mean."

"I sure as hell can be mean. In case you forgot, she left me, us, and everyone else behind." I point between the three us. Bo's just standing there, quiet as can be.

"I know, but that was a long time ago. Ash has her reasons and I've forgiven her."

I hate that she still calls her Ash. That started as my nickname for her and everyone else picked up on it; hearing it only adds salt to an old wound.

"Well, I haven't," I state firmly.

"But Clay-"

"Hey, let's go grab food like we had planned, enough of this," Bo interrupts and I'm glad. I didn't want to keep bickering with Sunny.

"That sounds like a great idea, man." I clap Bo on the shoulder and make my way past him toward the door.

I had originally planned to meet them both at the bar to grab food, but decided last minute to swing by Sunny's and offer her a ride. Seeing Bo's truck here struck me as odd when I pulled in, but then I figured he was doing what I had planned and was offering too. We both had to drive past to get to the bar. It only made sense to stop.

Sunny sighs as she grabs her things and the three of us head out with no more talk of Ashton Carpenter, and that's just fine with me.

8

Ashton

The day has come. I have no choice but to call Aunt Lynne. I sigh as I look at myself in the mirror, giving myself the once over.

I'm dressed in a bright pink sleeveless blouse, black slacks, and black stiletto heels. My blonde hair is pulled up in a tight bun. I completed my look with a full face of makeup, smoky eyes, and bright pink lip gloss. I like making a bold statement at the office. I have to if I want to survive in the world of fashion. It's a tough career being a merchandiser for big companies, and I have seen firsthand that they have no problem replacing employees who don't fit the part.

As I stare at my reflection a minute longer, I realize I look nothing like the Carolina girl I once was. I also notice the dark circles trying to peak through the foundation I've applied. They weren't there before. I chuck it up to stress and walk away.

On my way out of my room, I grab my cell off of the night

stand and pull up my aunt's name. I say a silent prayer and hit call. It rings only once before she answers.

"Good mornin' sugar, what has you calling so early?"

Hearing her voice is both soothing and stressful. When did it become stressful to talk to my aunt? Oh right, when I left.

"Morning. I figured I'd give you a call before I head into work." I don't know why I delay the reason for my call, but I do.

"Ah, how's that fancy career treating ya?"

I smile at her words. She's never understood my desire to go into fashion, yet she never put it down or discouraged me. She always told me to follow my dream, whatever it may be, and to excel at it.

"It's going good, I really like what I'm currently working on."

"That's nice, dear, I'm glad."

There's a silence between us. I know she's waiting on me to say why I really called so I man up and say what I need to say.

"So… the reason I'm calling is because I guess I have to come back to Nebo." I swallow thickly. I can feel myself start to sweat. That's the last thing I need, my makeup melting before I even step outside. I will myself to calm down and wait for her response.

"Mmhm, I see," she replies.

"I can't afford to live down here alone. My pay nowhere near pays all the bills," I tell her as I pour a cup of coffee and add vanilla creamer. I smile at my actions; my aunt would balk at that. No one drinks coffee in Nebo with cream. It's black and strong or nothing at all.

"Well, I guess you need to get packin'. Do you need me to come down there to help you move back?"

"No, no, I should be able to do it on my own. I'm going to sell the big stuff, that'll give me some extra cash too."

"Alright then. You have a place here to stay, but you'll have to pay your dues. No living for free, Ashton," she tells me sternly.

"Of course not. I don't expect you to support me and hey, would you mind keeping an ear out for any places hiring?"

Yep, there goes the last bit of my pride. Nebo most certainly won't need or want my degree. I'll have to travel for that kind of work, but job hunting will have to wait until I'm back, settled, and have saved for a bit.

My new goal is to save until I can move to a bigger city and then leave that small town behind…again.

"When should I expect you?" my aunt asks, bringing me back to the present

"By the end of the month, I have to tie up some loose ends first."

"I'll get your room ready." Aunt Lynne pauses a moment. "And Ashton, you're gonna have to hold your head up and put on your thick skin. Many are still displeased with you. I suggest when you get here, you start making amends."

I squeeze my eyes shut to prevent the tears. "Yes, ma'am." It's all I can say before we hang up.

She ain't wrong, and that's what scares me the most about returning back to my small town.

9

Ashton

I've managed to pack up the entire house, minus Brody's office. I was hoping he would stop by and do it himself, but no such luck. I have to be out of this place in two weeks and I can't hold off any longer. I grab a trash bag and make my way to his office.

Most of the furniture in the house has been sold so that gives me a little bit of cushion money. Lord knows I'm going to need it. Between lawyer fees and the gas to get back to North Carolina, I probably won't have much left.

Luckily my job is going to allow me to try working remotely as a trial. I'll have to go to Florida once a month; however, I'm grateful they are even offering me this. Now I just hope the internet will be strong enough since I'll be living in the middle of nowhere.

I haven't told Sunny I'm coming home yet. I want to wait as long as possible before telling her. It's not that I don't trust her with not telling people I was returning. I just know she would accidentally slip in conversation and it would spread like wild fire. I have asked my aunt not to tell many people. I don't want to be the source of gossip before I even got back.

I reach the door and turn the cold knob. His scent engulfs me as I walk in and turn on the light. A pang of hurt and loss comes over me even though I know this is for the best. It still fucking stings though, knowing I did this to myself. I shouldn't have married him.

I walk up to the two paintings he had hung on the wall and the few knickknacks he had on the book shelf. Things I had gotten him over the few years we were together. I toss them straight in the trash. He won't be needing them and neither will I. I decide to save his desk for last, and after my findings, I wish it was the first place I had packed up.

I find statements from his credit cards, completely maxed out. Statements showing spa charges in Miami. I know damn well he didn't take me to any spa. Who was he taking? I find letters from loan companies and how behind he is on those payments. Some of these loans I didn't even know about; so much for him doing good in the hotels and casinos. I realize now that maybe I didn't really know my husband. I grow more upset with each piece of paper I pick up, that is until I grab a lease agreement. It's for a high-rise condo in Miami. It wouldn't have been a huge deal to me since he told me he moved into another place. It's the names on the lease that have me seeing red.

The first name on the lease is Trisha Mabry, a mutual friend of ours. Brody is the second name.

They. Moved. In. Together. What the fuck? I sink down into his chair.

How did I not see this coming?

I close my eyes and think back to times we all hung out

together. Brody and Trisha got along, and occasionally I would see maybe what some would call flirting. I chucked it up to us having too many drinks.

This lease, however, leads me to believe that they are more than friends. Trisha had an apartment in Hollywood that was close to work. There's no way she would just move so Brody had a roommate.

I shake my head. I'm such a fool. He told me he wasn't ready to settle down, but boy, he sure settled in with Trisha right under my nose.

I swipe up all the papers. I'll be delivering these to Glenda. If I'm lucky she can get me more money. No more playing nice. I don't give a damn anymore.

———

After stewing for a little bit, I decide *fuck it* and called Sunny. I don't know why but something inside of me snapped in that room. I was never one to put up with being treated less than I deserved, then I moved here and was lost. I adjusted and kept my mouth shut just to please strangers. God, I hate myself. I vow right then and there while waiting for Sunny to answer that I will not be taking any more crap and that I will start living for me.

It's loud in the background when Sunny finally answers. "Hey, Ash!" she yells, and I have to pull the phone away.

"Hey, where are you?" She's probably at some bar or night club if I had to guess.

"I'm out at a brewery listening to some live cover band. They are great! I can't wait to bring you to see them."

"Sounds like you're having a good time. I can call you later." I don't want to impose on her night.

"No way, what's up? You sound… different."

How can she tell, especially with all the noise?

"There's just so much, but really, we can talk tomorrow."

"Hold on a sec, Bo, I'll be right back in," I hear Sunny yell. She's out with Bo and probably Clay. Ugh.

The sound on the other line goes quiet, and for a second I think she might have hung up, I pull the phone away to check.

"Sunny?"

"Okay, spill; what's going on?"

"Brody has so much debt. I went to clean out his office and found mounds of bills and notices."

"Wow. Aren't ya glad you are getting a divorce now?"

I sigh. "That's not all. Brody leased a condo in Miami." I take a deep breath. "With a friend of mine who happens to be a girl, and I found spa receipts."

"Whoah! What an asshole."

"I know, I know." I don't know what else to say.

"I'm double glad you are getting a divorce."

"Me too. I know now it's for the best."

"Want me to come down and kick his ass?"

I laugh; leave it to her to make me feel better about my shitty situation. "No, I'm good, besides I'm coming home." I decide to just blurt it out and wait.

"WHAT?! Did you say you were coming home? Oh my gosh!!" She practically screams into the phone and once again I have to pull it away from my ear.

"Calm down, girl, and yes, I'm coming home. Don't be telling no-one though."

"Why not? They're gonna find out sooner or later, Ash. Let's pull the band aid off and move on."

"Just not yet, I'm not ready. Baby steps… okay?" I plead, hoping she'll understand.

"Fine, I'll hold my tongue, but only until you get here."

"That's all I ask." I'm grateful she is willing to keep this between us. I just hope she doesn't slip beforehand.

"I'm coming!" Sunny shouts to someone before turning her attention back to me. "Listen, I'm really excited about what you just told me and also pissed off at Brody, but I gotta get back inside. Everyone is lookin' for me."

"Go. We'll talk soon."

"K. Bye, Ash." Sunny hangs up before I even get to say goodbye. That's just like her too. She doesn't drag ass. I can't wait to see her either. It's been far too long.

10

Ashton

The drive home seems to be the longest drive of my life. I've been on the road since five am. and it's nearly five pm now. I stopped a few times to stretch my legs, get food, and use the bathroom. Even though I know I'm making good time, it still seems as though time is creeping by.

The mountains have started to come into view now, and it'll be at least another twenty-five or thirty minutes more of driving through the winding roads that'll lead up to my aunt's property.

I packed everything I owned into my small SUV. I didn't have much when all was said and done, mostly clothes and shoes that will stand out like a sore thumb when I get to where I'm going.

The closer to Morganton I get, the more I start to panic about making it to Nebo. I have to remind myself to take deep breaths as I hit North Carolina. My mind is made up, no turning back now, even if I am scared to death of returning.

Thankfully driving through town is a breeze. No one seems to stop and stare. Then again, no one knows my vehicle. I got rid of my old pick up and opted for something with better gas mileage. It is nothing fancy, even with my tinted windows. I am glad for that too. Not that my SUV stands out or anything, but this is a small town and there's always someone who notices when someone passes through. At least that's the way it used to be. Maybe times have changed. I doubt it though.

As I take the road leading up to my aunt's, I put the window down just a little bit to breathe in the fresh air. Oh, how I've missed this.

I take the curve and see the street sign for Aunt Lynne's. Firefly Lane. I smile, almost excited to see fireflies at night, something I haven't seen since I left. I turn up her driveway and take the gravel path on up to the house. She has a creek that runs along the western side of the property. Driving slowly, I can hear the water flowing and it almost feels like home.

As her house comes into view, I get teary eyed. I haven't been back to this place since I left seven years ago. This is home. I shouldn't have stayed away so long, but I just couldn't bring myself to do it.

I put the car in park and quickly get out of my SUV. I take a deep breath in. The air is so much fresher up here; living in the city sure doesn't smell this good.

I hear the screen door and turn my attention toward the house. Aunt Lynne is making her way down the steps to greet me. I half run and throw my arms around her immediately.

"Well, hello to you too, dear." She laughs. "How was the drive?"

"Long." I pull back and take her in. She's aged since I last got to see her. She came to Florida about two year ago. It was a quick trip because she really couldn't stand Brody.

"Let's get you unloaded. I got dinner cooking." She makes her way toward my vehicle, but I stop her.

"No, ma'am, go back in. I'll get this stuff."

"Alright then, Ashton, I'll be in the kitchen."

I smile as I watch her retreat back into the house. I walk to the other side of my car and look out at the land. Aunt Lynne sits on twenty acres. Mostly woodland. You can't even see the neighbors' houses. It's nice and secluded up here. I am hoping to fly under the radar for a little bit.

I start to unload my car and notice the slight chill in the air, not too cold for a summer night, though it's something else I'll have to adjust too. It's also not humid like Florida; my hair will be happy about that.

It takes me no time to unload. I am shown to my room, the same room that was mine when I lived here. Part of me had hoped she had renovated some and that I would have the spare room, but no such luck.

Being back in that room takes me back to better days. Days that might have continued if I didn't leave.

"Nope, not going there, Ashton. You had your reasons. You left to save Clay," I say out loud as I put the last of my shoes away.

"Ashton! Dinner!" Aunt Lynne hollers from the kitchen, just like old times.

"Be right there!" I yell back as I get up and close the closet door.

Dinner is waiting on the table when I come out of my room. Roasted chicken with green beans and sweet potatoes. I moan as I take the first bite. I haven't had a southern dinner in so long. "I've missed your cooking,"

"I'm sure you have. Lord knows that husband didn't like your cooking."

"Ha, his loss."

It's true. Brody missed out on some good comfort food. He didn't like anything I made. He said it wasn't his style, whatever that meant. Most nights we ate separately and it usually involved take out or a microwave kind of dinner. The nights we were together consisted of dinner out at a restaurant. He never even cared to try anything I made while I was in the culinary academy. All the signs were there, yet I didn't see them.

"The Neon Moon could use a waitress. I told Bo you would stop in tomorrow for an application. He unlocks the door at noon."

Man, she wastes no time; then again, she was never one that did.

"Thank you for checking for me. Isn't he mad at me though?" I am afraid Bo would let me fill out the entire application and then rip it up right in front of me.

"Why would he be mad, dear? He needs a waitress and you need a job."

"I guess."

The rest of dinner is eaten in silence and that's perfectly okay with me.

11

Ashton

I wake extra early just so I can have a cup of coffee on the front porch. The hummingbirds are flittering around the feeder that my aunt keeps filled for them. I sit there taking it all in. I have missed so much. You definitely don't see any hummingbirds in south Florida. I take a sip and close my eyes. The creek behind the house is flowing and there are birds chirping away. It's peaceful up here.

The screen door opening causes me to startle and pop my eyes open.

"Good mornin', Ashton," Aunt Lynne says as she takes the rocker next to me.

"Morning,"

"Did ya sleep okay?"

"I did, thank you." It was probably the best sleep I've had in a long time.

"I'll be headed into town in about an hour to open up the

bakery if ya want a ride."

"I think I'll follow behind you, if that's okay." It's not really, but I won't tell her that.

She just nods and sips her coffee. I dread going into town and seeing people. I know I need to put my big girl panties on and handle it, but I still dread it.

———

I follow her into town an hour later, exactly as Aunt Lynne had said. Walking into the bakery causes me to still. The smell of apple everything hangs in the air. The scent takes me back immediately to Clay. His farm, being in the bakery together. It's almost too much; I have to force myself to continue walking further in.

My aunt goes about getting everything ready as I sit at one of the tables. I go about checking my emails, trying to stay busy until I have to leave to go to the bar. I plan to leave as close to noon as possible since the bar is just around the corner and I'd like to get there without being seen.

"Alright, Aunt Lynne, I'm gonna head on over to see Bo."

"K," is all I hear from the back; she sounds like her head is in the oven so I leave her to it and head out.

———

As I stand outside the bar, it occurs to me that I've never stepped foot in The Neon Moon. I take a deep breath as I pull on the handle. "Here goes nothing."

I'm not sure what I am expecting, but the view in front of me is not it. I take in the bar's appearance; it gives off a dark and mysterious vibe. There's posters all around, but aside from that it's pretty plain.

It's completely quiet and Bo is nowhere in sight. I rub my now clammy hands down my pants. I had a hard time deciding what to wear today. In the end I went with navy pants and a cream short sleeve top. I curled my hair and did my face up with natural tones and navy eyeliner to make my blue eyes pop.

I hesitate before walking further in, my nude heels announcing my presence. I should have worn flats.

After another minute and no Bo, I bravely call out, "Hello?" And then wait.

"Be right out," comes from behind two swinging doors that are located directly next to the bar.

I can feel myself start to sweat. I haven't seen Bo, one of my best friends, since graduation night. What a shit person I was, still am.

Bo walks through the doors not even a minute later, bringing me out of my head and back to the present. I take him in. He hasn't changed at all, yet he has. He's no longer a baby face blue eyed cutie anymore; he's more man now, and light stubble covers his jaw. His dirty blonde hair is cut shorter than I remember, but it suits him.

"Well, I'll be damned," he says as he tosses the towel on the bar.

I don't know what to say to that, so I stay quiet and offer a small smile.

"Ashton Carpenter, I really can't believe you are here, standing in my bar."

I let out a small laugh. "Well, I am."

"Looks like I'm out a hundred bucks." He slaps his hand on the bar, laughing.

He's what? I'm confused, "I'm sorry?" My eye brow raise in question to what he just said.

"I'm sorry. Clay and I made a bet. I bet you wouldn't show up here."

What the hell? They've taken bets out on me, just wonderful. I cringe at the thought.

"Oh." It's barely a whisper and I'd really like to shrink and disappear.

"Really, I'm sorry, Ashton. It was all in good fun, I swear."

I wave him off. "You don't have to explain."

"So… Your aunt says you're lookin' for a job."

"I am."

"All jokes aside, I need someone. Someone I can depend on. If you're up for it, I'll grab an application out of the office." I follow his hand as he hooks a thumb over his shoulder, gesturing to back behind the swinging doors.

"Yes, please, that would be great." I know what he was hinting at and decide not to play into it. I just need this job so I can focus on the bigger plan.

"Give me a sec." Bo turns and walks back to where he had come from when he came out to greet me. I'm thankful for the breather, as I need to calm myself and remember that I'm a professional who doesn't cave under pressure.

Bo comes back out with a paper attached to a clipboard. He hands it to me along with a pen.

"You can fill it out here, find a seat. I got work to do, just holler when you're done."

"Thank you," I tell him as I hold my head up high, taking the clipboard from his hands. I walk over to one of the many tables and sit down.

I look around; the bar has several square shaped tables like the one I am sitting at. Each one seats four. There's six booths, three lining each side of the building. There's a small area that looks to be for dancing and a makeshift stage that would fit a small band or maybe a DJ.

I can do this, I tell myself as I begin to fill out the application. *I can do this.*

Ten minutes later I have it completed.

"Here's to hoping he hires me," I whisper as I walk back up to the bar.

"Bo, I've finished."

He comes out from the back and smiles. I return the smile. Maybe he doesn't hate me after all. As he takes the clipboard he asked, "So how have you been?"

"Umm, I've been…" Shit, how do I word this, what do I say? "Well, I've been better." No sense in lying.

"I heard you were getting a divorce. That sucks."

"No, it's okay, we weren't meant to be." I shrug my shoulders. It's a fact that I'm learning to accept as each day goes by.

Bo looks over the application quietly so I wait in silence. Waiting is not one of my best qualities. Especially since I'm waiting for Bo to chew me up and spit me out.

When he finally clears his throat, my heart rate picks up.

"You don't have waitressing or bartending skills, but you can be taught." He eyes me cautiously.

"I'm willing to learn." I stand taller, hoping he'll see how serious I am about wanting this job. He says nothing, just nods and looks back to the application. The air between us is nearly suffocating and I'm almost ready to bolt when he speaks again.

"I suppose I can give you a job, I'll see how you do."

I'm shocked! "Really?!"

"Yes, I'll try you out, some nights are fast paced and you gotta be able to keep up."

"Okay." I reach my hand out to shake his, but he just looks at it and then back to me.

"Ashton, I'm giving you a job, but you are gonna have to earn your keep."

"Yes, I under-" Before I can finish, he interrupts me.

"People aren't going to like you, and I won't stand for problems here, ya understand?"

"Yes, sir."

I realize that he's serious and he needs his place to run smoothly. I don't plan to engage in drama. In fact, I hope to keep my head down and just do my work.

"Good, you can start tomorrow at noon then."

I smile big; he's really giving me a chance.

I take a step to hug him, but stop short when he holds his hand out, stopping me.

"Now, Ashton, one last thing. I'm glad your back and all, but don't be wasting my time if you're planning on taking off again with no notice."

His words sting. I open my mouth to reply but can't bring myself to respond. Instead, I nod my head.

Bo nods his head once and turns toward the bar; when he reaches the doors, he turns to look back at me. He eyes me up and down and for a moment I'm a little uncomfortable.

"Jeans and a t-shirt are dress code. You'll want to lose those things too." Bo pauses then points to my heels.

"We don't do that here." He waves his hand up and down at my attire.

"Noted."

With that, he turns and walks through the doors without so much as a goodbye.

I exhale. That wasn't terribly bad. It could have gone worse. I dab at my head slightly at the sweat that has formed and make my way to the front door.

As I go to push it open, the door is pulled opened, causing me to nearly stumble into the person on the other side. Out of instinct I throw my hands out to steady me, and they land on someone's chest. This is embarrassing. When I look up, my greatest fear is standing on the other side holding the door open.

Clay Williams.

12

Clay

When I pull open the door to Bo's, I'm not expecting a woman to practically fall into my arms. Once the blonde is steady, I get a look at her and grow cold. Ashton fucking Carpenter. She is clearly shocked to see me as well. I watch as her hand leaves my chest and fly to her chest. It's a sure sign that I did, in fact, startle her. By the look on her face, I can tell she wasn't expecting to run into me of all people, but then she goes and shocks me when she opens her mouth.

"Um… hi," she says sheepishly.

Is she really trying to say hello to me? I say nothing in return; instead I just glare at her and it makes her shift nervously. I scan her up and down. What the fuck is she even wearing and what's all over her face? I let out a sarcastic laugh. I can't help it, but yeah, I fucking laugh.

That must piss her off a little because her hands instantly

move to her hips and she gives me a questioning look that says *What the fuck is so funny?*

Ashton's blue eyes staring back at me causes the last bit of my cold heart to snap off. She's got no right to even look at me.

"What the hell are you looking at?"

"Wha... what?" she stutters. She's caught off guard by how rude I was. Good, because there's more where that came from.

"You heard me, Ashton. Don't fucking look at me like that. Not with your prim and proper clothes and too good attitude." I'm growing angrier by the minute. I need her ass to move so I can get to where I was going, to see Bo.

"I didn't look at you like anything, Clay."

Ashton looks down as she says my name. I hate hearing my name leave her lips. Lips I used to kiss. Lips that used to tell me they loved me. Lips that betrayed me. Fuck!

"Oh yeah, that's right, I was never nothin' to you. Makes sense seeing as how you up and left because you were too good for me."

Ashton's mouth drops open as I continue on my rant, not caring one bit.

"Did you expect a welcome home party? One full of roses and happiness? I'm here to tell you that you ain't gettin' all that. You're not liked anymore. No. One. Wants. You. Here." I say each word slowly. It's a dick move, but I don't regret it, not one bit. I'm mad and Ashton's just standing there taking it.

She finally looks back up to me; tears are evident in her eyes. Good, I hope she feels some sort of remorse. She caused me so much pain when she left me that I thought I'd never recover.

Just then I hear Bo come through the doors. I turn in his direction as he looks between the two of us.

"Fuck," he says as he wipes his face while walking up to us.

Ashton takes a step back as if she's afraid to be too close to me or him.

"What's going on, Clay?" Bo glances at Ashton as she tries to wipe under her eyes quickly.

"I was just letting Ashton here know that she's not welcomed home."

"Come on now, Clay. Don't pay any attention to her." Bo curses under his breath and turns to Ashton.

"Ashton, I think it is best you go now."

I watch as she flinches in response and nods her head.

"That's right, Ashton, run along, it's what you're good at." I raise my voice, not caring that it causes her to jump.

I need to get out of here. I haven't seen red like this in a long time. I turn to go, and suddenly remember Bo lost his bet over Ashton.

"By the way, I want my hundred in twenties. Bet you weren't expecting to lose a bet over her." I point at Ashton then let go of the handle to the door I still had in my hand.

As I storm toward my pickup I hear Bo start to holler. I look back and see Ashton standing there, head hanging low. Fuck her.

I open my truck door and climb in. I fucking hate Ashton and hate that she is back here. Grabbing my door to shut it, I decide to get one more jab in.

"I hope you didn't hire her. She'll cause you to lose business."

I don't miss the sob that escapes her as I slam the door. Part of me feels like scum for that last bit, yet I'm too mad to care. I put the truck in drive and high tail it out of the lot, refusing to let myself look in the rearview mirror.

Ashton

I try to control the tears but they just keep coming. Bo tries to apologize some for Clay's outburst, but I won't allow him to take fault. It is a nice gesture and all, but still doesn't help the fact that Clay hates me. I expected him to, but the reality is worse than I could have ever pictured.

Bo had warned me. People were going to be mean. I know I deserve some of it, yet when Clay said I would cause Bo to lose patrons, it hurt. I don't want to be the reason he loses customers.

I put my car in park and jump out immediately. I unstrap my heels and step out of them, leaving them right there on the ground. I don't even bother to head for the house. There's only one place I want to be. I take off around the back of the house and head up the slope toward the woods. Hiking through this part of the land has always brought me a sense of comfort. Being in these woods reminds me of simpler times.

I walk a little way in and plop down on a patch of fallen leaves. The sun has peeked through and luckily, the leaves are dry. Though, I don't think I would have bothered to care if they were wet. With my arms on my knees, I hold my head in my hands and cry. I cry for everything I've messed up in life. I thought me leaving was a good thing. "I'm such a mess," I say out loud.

I take a deep breath and lay back. I close my eyes and let the warmth takeover me and then for the first time in a long time, I allow myself to drift back over memories of Clay and I.

———

Ten years prior

Aunt Lynne's land goes on and on. Most of it's untouched by man. There's a mixture of evergreens and maple trees throughout. Clay and I would trek through it for what felt like hours until our legs were sore, then we'd plop on down on the moss and leaves. Going hiking through the property after the first frost was our favorite. It was the first sign that colder days were coming when all the leaves had started falling.

It was beautiful, as if it was just the two of us in the world. Nothing else existed in those woods, just Clay and I. It's the way I liked it to be. I didn't have to think about real life. I could shut off from the world and just be.

One October day, something shifted in those woods. It was the day Clay and I had been laying on a flannel throw blanket that we placed on the ground, staring up at the tall pines.

"Stay still," Clay had said to me.

He leaned over slightly and kissed me on the lips. I can still remember the way my stomach did somersaults when he pulled back and gave me a nervous smile. I hadn't expected him to kiss me. Hell, we were fifteen years old and had not the first clue about love.

However, when he kissed me that day in the woods, I let the butterflies in my stomach take flight for the first time. I had no idea at that very moment what that kiss meant, I just knew I wanted more.

Clay said nothing after he kissed me, he just pulled back and tucked some stray hairs behind my ear.

We eventually made our way back out of our bubble in the woods and back to reality.

After that day though, every time we hiked the land, we kissed. Stolen kisses here and there, soft kisses, deep and passionate kisses. We explored each other's mouths with a fire I didn't know existed until the day his lips met mine.

We'd always been together, Clay and Ashton, also dubbed CLASH by Bo and some other friends of ours. We laughed it off, but the name stuck. They'd holler *CLASH* in the hallways at school and everyone knew it meant me and Clay.

The two of us often held hands, yet it wasn't in a romantic way. Clay held my hand whenever he knew I was overwhelmed or becoming upset. He would just quietly slide his hand into mine and rub his thumb over the back of my hand. It worked every time. If I had tears, he embraced me and held me in his arms. I'd lean my head on his chest, allowing the beating from his heart to soothe me. In a way, Clay had always been my lifeline.

———

I sigh, thinking back over our moments here. We had some special moments that I wouldn't trade for the world, but people change and time changes everything. However, I'm determined to hold my head up high and not let Clay destroy what's left of me. I will just have to learn to ignore him and his angry words. Standing up, I wipe off the leaves that have stuck to me and make my way back to the house.

I have several missed calls and one text from Sunny.

GIRL DON'T YA DARE LISTEN TO THAT BOY!

I have to laugh. Of course she would find out that Clay was a jerk earlier. I bet Bo called her to do damage control. I pick up and dial her number.

"Ashton! You answered!"

I giggle. "Um…yeah?"

"I thought maybe Clay sent you fleeing again."

Ouch. I so deserved that one, yet shrug it off and try not to take offense.

"No, I just walked Aunt Lynne's to clear my head. He would have to do more than throw words at me to chase me off."

"Oh good! So… how was it seeing Bo? Isn't he looking nice these days?"

"He looks like Bo, just older."

"Yeah, I guess. He said you start tomorrow? Are you nervous?"

Ha. Nervous is an understatement. "I am. Shoot, that reminds me. Do you have a pair of jeans I could borrow?" I don't own jeans these days. "It would only be until I can find time to go shopping."

"Sure, why don't you come over? We can catch up and you can raid my closet."

"Sounds like a plan. I'll see you soon."

We hang up and I head back out feeling much better than I have in a while. I almost feel free.

14

Ashton

My first few days at The Neon Moon go surprisingly well. Bo is only letting me work day shifts and no weekends. It's both annoying and a relief. It's annoying because I'd like to make more in tips. It's also a relief because I have been able to stay under the radar and haven't ran into Clay again. I'm not sure if he's avoiding the place because of me or not; either way, I'm glad.

I'm wiping down a table when Madi walks in. She does the night shift here.

"Hey, Ashton," she calls out as she sets her stuff behind the bar.

"Hey, there," I wave and continue about my way.

I have nothing against Madi; she was always kind to me when we were in school. I'm just not ready to make conversation.

"I hear Bo might start you this weekend."

What?? I look at her confused. "Huh?"

"It's a big weekend here, we are gonna need extra hands."

"What's happening this weekend?"

"Oh you know… it's Clay's birthday. Bo always throws him a killer party here." Madi flips her blonde curls back over her shoulder and looks at me like I should already know this.

Clays birthday, how could I forget it? My heart sinks at the thought. Surely Bo is not letting me work it. He said himself he didn't want no drama.

I say nothing to Madi regarding Clay. There's no reason to. Right now the only thing haunting me is why hasn't Bo mentioned this to me? Maybe Madi misunderstood him. I sure hope that's the case.

Another twenty minutes goes by before my shift finally comes to an end. I was relieved each time that Bo came out and didn't mention this weekend to me. My hope dwindles though when I reach for my purse and see Bo come through the doors.

"Hey, Ashton, let me walk you out. "

He looks to Madi. "Take over until I come back in."

She nods and waves goodbye to me. I smile in return even though I'm starting to panic on the inside. So much for getting out of here without Bo talking to me.

We walk in silence until we reach my SUV. Bo stands next to me not saying a word. I guess it's up to me to break the ice.

"So?" I question him.

"Yeah, um… listen, this weekend is a big one for the bar. I'm gonna need you Saturday, all day, open to close."

Way to skirt around it, Bo.

I nod. "I've never done a weekend here; you sure you want me to start on such a busy one?"

I'm hoping to, I don't know, maybe convince him that this isn't a good idea. I have my hands in my back pockets, fingers crossed. Childish, I know, but I'm desperate.

"Yeah, I've thought it over and decided if you're gonna make it in my bar, this weekend will be the ultimate test."

That fucker. I could scream. He's doing this on purpose. I can't hold my tongue.

"So having me work Clay's birthday bash or whatever you wanna call it, is my test? How fair is that? Clay hates me."

I stop and throw my head back when I hear my southern accent slip out. When I left, I worked hard to suppress it and sound less like me. Looking back, I realize that was pretty dumb.

"Now, Ashton," Bo pauses. "Wait, how did you know it was his party?"

"Madi might have already told me." I roll my eyes. Seriously that's what he's focusing on?

Bo curses. "Damn it, Madi can never keep her mouth shut."

I turn my head to the side. "I really have to work it?"

"Yes. Let's face it, you need to work some weekends. I know you aren't making jack during the week. Remember, I write your paycheck."

He's not wrong, but I still don't like the idea of working Clay's birthday.

"Clay won't want me there, Bo."

"That's where you're wrong. I asked him if he minded, he said some stuff I won't repeat, but in the end he agreed to be on his best behavior."

"Oh."

"Besides, you'll most likely be too busy with the guests. Chances are you may not see him at all."

I sigh. "Fine, okay. But if he-"

Bo cuts me off. "If he gets nasty, I'll send you home with full pay and tips."

Hmm… that's not a bad trade off since I need the money and all. I reach my hand out to Bo. "Deal."

"Deal," Bo replies.

———

On the weekends, the waitresses wear cut off shorts and tanks with their cowboy boots. Madi said it brought in better tips so here I am in a pair of denim cut offs and a white tank top that's tied in a knot. Once again, I had to raid Sunny's closet. I pull my hair to the side and braid it. I go with just a little makeup, eye liner and mascara only. I don't want to draw more attention than necessary. I'm trying my hardest to blend in, especially after Bo's comment about me. I slide on my boots that Aunt Lynne had saved and kept in my closet all these years. She told me that she knew I would need them one day. Damn her for being right.

Standing, I give myself the once over. I adjust my tank slightly. I don't want my boobs popping out, that would surely draw attention.

Here goes nothing.

15

Ashton

The bar has been transformed completely. There's black table cloths draped over the tables and black balloons everywhere. Who is this Clay? I've never known him to be a big party boy. Then again, I don't know this Clay. I remind myself of this fact as I continue unloading bottles of whiskey and tequila.

At six pm on the dot, people begin to trickle in. Bo has me walking around with appetizers on a tray. It's easy, people don't have to acknowledge me, just take one and go. I can handle this all night. I like being invisible.

After a while, people suddenly start hootin' and hollerin'. I turn my attention toward all the noise to see what the fuss is about. Should have known it is Clay, but nothing could have prepared me for seeing him dressed the way he is. I find myself staring at him, No, scratch that, I'm not just staring. My mouth is agape as I take him in from head to toe.

He has on gray cowboy boots, followed by black jeans that seem to fit him just right. His black button up shirt has me wanting to rip it off of him. The two top buttons are left undone, exposing a teaser of what lies underneath that shirt. He finishes his look with a black cowboy hat. It is enough to make a grown woman drool.

I shouldn't be thinking these thoughts, but hot damn, Clay is sexy even if he is a jerk to me. I feel my face heat at those thoughts. He smiles at something someone says and it's nearly my undoing. His smile has always been my favorite thing about him. He is gorgeous when he smiles; his dimples appear, and I swear that alone is enough to make a girl's panties wet.

Clay continues to glance around the room, saying hello to friends, before his eyes land on mine. I watch as his smile falters for a second before he recovers it. People probably didn't even catch it, but I did. I quickly cast my eyes down and turn away.

I knew he wouldn't be happy to see me, but it still hurts a little. The boy who was once my everything is now a man I don't even know. I make my way further from him and continue serving people until my tray is empty.

As I enter through the doors, I hear Bo and Madi in a heated discussion. I don't want to interrupt; however, I am not sure what Bo wants me to serve next.

"Sorry to interrupt, but what would you like me to bring out to the guests now?"

Both Madi and Bo stop and look at me. Well, this isn't awkward at all.

Bo looks at the prep table and grabs a tray.

"Here, take these directly to Clay, they are his tequila shots."

"Um… are you sure that's a good idea?" I know for a fact it is not a good idea. Not at all.

"Just do it, Ashton!" Bo snaps.

I'm taken aback; he has never snapped at me, ever.

"Shit. I'm sorry, please, just take these out." I can tell he feels bad for yelling so I nod my head and take the tray from him.

As I make my way out, I remind myself that I can do this. He'll probably pretend I'm not even there. I look around the bar until I spot Clay.

I walk up to him surrounded by a small group of people. Claire, a girl we went to high school with, has her arms wrapped around his with a big ol' smile on her face.

For some reason this irks me. I try to brush it off. I'm not a jealous person and have absolutely zero reason to be.

Get it together, Asthon.

I walk directly up and smile slightly as I present the tray full of liquor to the birthday boy. Clay glares at me for a moment; his stare lets me know I'm not welcome. I glance away, hoping he'll hurry and take the shots. The faster the tray gets unloaded, the quicker I can get the hell away from him.

Clay clears his throat, causing me to look back at him. He's smiling again as he starts handing shots out.

"Alright, ya'll, I declare a toast." He looks directly at me as he hands Claire the last shot. I turn to go; however, Clay has other plans. As he calls out my name, I pause and look at him.

"Ashton, why don't you stick around for my toast? It's dedicated to you."

People around us do several things all at once. Some gasp, some snicker like Claire, and some flat out whisper, "Here we go."

I feel my face turn red, yet I can't force my feet to walk away before this situation gets worse.

"To Ashton," Clay raises his drink. "To the girl who left me in the middle of the night right after we had sex for the first time." Clay downs his shot and when he finishes, he's no longer smiling at me. In fact, he looks mad as hell as he glares at me. His deep blue eyes penetrate me. I look away quickly, but I catch the tic in his jaw.

People burst into laughter at Clay's words. The air is so thick, I will it to suffocate me. No such luck because I drop the tray I was holding, which causes more laughter.

I quickly bend down to grab the tray and make a bee-line for the double doors, my only savior.

Once behind them, the first tear slips. I try to calm my nerves by taking deep breaths. I will not cry tonight. Not over him.

If only he knew how much that night really meant to me, maybe he wouldn't have been so mean just then.

———

Graduation night
7 years prior

I gave myself to Clay on graduation night. We were both virgins, and even though we had fooled around plenty, we were nervous.

"Ashton, are you sure about this?" Clay asked hovering above me, his arms on each side of me as he held his weight off of me.

Leaning up to kiss him softly, I said, "I am sure."

I was trembling slightly, but managed to keep a smile on my face as he lined himself up at my entrance.

"I love you, Ashton,"

"I love you too," I whispered.

As he pushed into me, I gasped and squeezed my eyes shut. It hurt. There was a burning sensation and it stung.

Clay stopped moving, "Does it hurt?"

"Just a little, keep moving."

It wasn't long before the burning was replaced with pleasure and as Clay finished, he kissed me. It was the most passionate kiss we ever shared. I don't know if it was because we were having sex for the first time, but it was definitely a kiss for the books and where my heart should have swelled with love, it was slowly dying instead.

Afterwards, we held each other for what seemed like hours. We looked at each other, kissed each other, and as he drifted to sleep, I knew it would be the last time he would see my eyes, the last time I would see his. What I was about to do would crush us both, but it had to be done.

When the sun started to rise, a sinking feeling began to form in my heart. Last night Clay was the perfect gentleman and everything about last night was amazing.

As I quietly slipped out of his window, I started to hate myself a little more. I'm a terrible person.

Little did he know, that when he would wake, he would lose me and everything that we had.

16

Clay

I realize I fucked up the minute the words leave my mouth. I just told everyone in the bar, which might as well equal all of Nebo, about Ashton and I. I hadn't told anyone about that night except Bo. I made him swear not to tell a soul or I'd cut his balls off. If only I had listened to my own words.

Claire is now all over me, telling me she can help me forget all about Ashton. Her blonde curls bounce off her shoulder with each move she makes. I don't doubt she could help me out and I will probably take her up on her offer later, after a few more drinks.

Sunny finds me and she looks pissed.

"Clay! Why you gotta be like this?"

I pretend to have no idea what she's talking about.

"Be like what?" I flash her my panty dropping smile. What? It's what Sunny often says about my smile.

Claire giggles and continues rubbing my arm. Her green eyes twinkle and she smiles like she just won a prize. Me being the prize. I watch as Sunny watches Claire movements. I see her nostrils flare and know she's fixing to go off.

"What are you laughin' at, Claire? Wait, don't bother telling me. Go on off somewhere. I'm trying to have a conversation with Clay and it sure don't involve you."

I cough, trying to cover the laugh that escapes my lips.

"Clay, are you gonna let her talk to me like that?" Claire looks up at me like I'm supposed to defend her. Sadly, for her, it doesn't work like that. Sunny is my friend and has been there for me through some dark times. Plus, the alcohol is kicking in. I could care less how Sunny talks to her.

"Well?" Claire demands, stomping her boots like a spoiled child.

I just shrug my shoulders. Claire huffs and storms away. Guess I won't be getting laid by her later. Oh well, I'm sure there will be someone else.

"Clay, look at me. I'm serious." Sunny's voice brings me back to reality and away from thinking with my dick.

"Okay… okay. I really didn't mean to blurt all that out. It just happened."

"I get it, you're angry with her, but letting shit out of the closet for the world to know ain't the way to deal with it. Especially when I didn't even know ya'll had sex." If I'm not mistaken, her words hold a hint of sadness or maybe jealously. Those same words take me by surprise too.

"Wait... Ashton never mentioned our one and only night together?" I'm baffled. How could she not tell her best friend?

"No, Clay, she didn't and she probably had her reasons. Reasons you just threw right out the window."

"Well, fuck. You know what? Oh, well," I say as I head off to where I know Ashton is. My mind is spinning. Was she that ashamed of sleeping me that she didn't tell anyone? What the fuck, not even Sunny, her very best friend. I'm fuming and know I need to calm down, but the tequila in me says *fuck it*.

I push through the swinging doors to see Ashton standing toward the back door with a tissue in her hand, blotting under her eyes. *Good, serves her right.*

Before I talk myself out it, I lay in on her, right then and there.

"So losing yourself to me meant that little to you, that you didn't even tell your best friend?"

She gasps, but I keep right on. Nope, she ain't getting off. Not this time.

"That night must have meant shit to you, that it caused you to just take off. Well guess what, you weren't that great either!"

Now that's a flat out lie. I don't know why I said it because that night had been so perfect. I could have died a happy man, but nope I was left confused and shattered.

She's full on crying now and I don't give a damn. This girl destroyed me. Now it's my turn to give her a dose of her own medicine.

"Tell me, Ashton, were you that ashamed of losing yourself to me that your only answer was to leave and pretend in never happened? Was that it?"

I stand there waiting. I want fucking answers.

"Wha—, no… it wasn't at all like that." Ashton hiccups.

I'm not buying what she's saying; she needs to give me more.

"Enlighten me, what was it? One minute we were getting lost in each other and the next I'm waking up alone."

Bo comes in as Ashton opens her mouth.

"Not now, Bo." I stare at him, challenging him.

Bo turns like he is going to leave, then stops short. "You okay, Ash?"

What the fuck? Why is everyone worried about her?

"She's fine, Bo, were just clearing some stuff up."

Bo glares at me. He's not happy and I really don't give a fuck.

"You got five minutes. Better clear it up fast."

As soon as Bo leaves, I dig again. "Well, I'm waiting and I don't have all night." I watch her. Maybe it's the liquor, but in this moment she looks innocent; her beautiful blue eyes haunt me. She looks like eighteen-year-old Ashton, the girl I was going to marry. I shake my head; screw those thoughts.

"Ashton, now," I snap, which causes her to jump.

She sighs before finally speaking. "I've never been ashamed of you, Clay Williams. I actually can't believe you would think that. I didn't want to share the best and worst day of my life with anyone else."

I hate the way she says my name as she looks defeated. I'm not sure what to say to what she just told me. The best and worst day of her life? What does that shit even mean?

"Care to explain that better?" I don't know why I want to know, but I do.

"Clay, that night meant everything to me. It couldn't have been more perfect, however, I also knew it would be our last night together. Yeah, it was selfish of me to do. I just wanted you to be my first before I let you go. I had to let you go, Clay."

She smiles a sad smile, one that doesn't reach her eyes.

I'm left speechless and more confused than ever.

Bo and Sunny come marching in. "You are a jerk, Clay," Sunny hollers as she goes straight to Ashton.

"Here," Bo says to Ashton as he hands her money.

What's up with that?

"Go on home. I'm sorry jackass—" he points to me —" just can't chill."

Ashton says nothing, just takes the cash and leaves through the back door. She doesn't even look back at me.

Maybe I screwed up a little, maybe she deserved it. Either way it happened. No going back. I run my fingers through my hair. It's my birthday and I'm going to celebrate.

I grab a bottle that's on the counter, open it, and take a swig.

"Happy Birthday to me," I say out loud and set off to find Claire.

Clay

My head is killing me as I sit at Bo's bar, trying to nurse my hangover. Last night after my confrontation with Ashton, I decided to get piss drunk. Something I don't really do these days. I ended up not going home with Claire and instead passed out in one of the booths here. Now here I am, with my head in my hands and a fucking aching back.

Bo emerges from the back and places a cup of coffee along with some toast in front of me.

"Here, eat."

I say nothing and just nod as I pick up the toast. He walks away and returns with a glass of water and two pills.

"Take these too."

"Yes, Mother." Seriously, he sounds like my ma right now.

"Watch it, you're still on my shit list."

I groan at that. I might have fucked up last night, I really don't remember to much though. I know I embarrassed Ashton and argued with her, but the details are a little fuzzy.

"Look, Clay, I think you need to talk to Ashton when your head is clear. You were a dick last night and way out of line. Yeah, she left us all and she sucks for that, but it's been several years now and you need to let that shit go and move on."

Bo's right, but I don't tell him that. I have too much pride to admit he may be right.

"She just came walkin' back to town in her prissy ass clothes, actin' like nothing happened. That's what sets me off the most. She is pretending."

"Dude, I'm sure she has her reasons and they must be big because not even Sunny knows shit."

I take a sip of my coffee. "I guess, man. It's just she had been my life. It fucking stings seeing her here." God, I sound like a pussy.

"Give Ashton some time, maybe she'll come around and explain, but you gotta stop fightin' with her every damn time you see her. All you're doing is making the situation worse."

We sit in silence for a little bit. I welcome it, I need to get my bearings straight. This is not who I am usually. I'm a happy guy who hardly loses it. I scratch my jaw and decide I can't let Ashton have this hold over me, not anymore.

When I get off shift, the first thing I do is go to the farm house and start the shower. I send a quick text to Blue to check in on how things were going. I like that I can count on him to run the farm when I'm on shift and can't always be there. Once the water is scalding hot, I strip off and get in, welcoming the stinging pain.

I get out of the shower and dry off, wrapping the towel

around my waist before heading back to my room. My phone buzzes, telling me I have a new text. There's two, one from Blue and one from Claire. I read the one from Blue first

All is good, crops are good.

I figured they would be. Things usually are. Now onto Claire's text.

Come on out to Hillside there's a bonfire tonight

I entertain the idea for a minute. I could go out for a little bit, have a beer, and head back. I have an early shift tomorrow and never screw off the night before. I lose the towel and start getting ready before I send Claire a response.

Be there in a bit

Hillside is full of people tonight; its nights like this that remind me of our high school days. We all use to pile in one of our trucks and head out. Occasionally we'd sneak beer from our parents' fridges. I smile at the memory. Those days of being sneaky are long gone.

I find Claire right away and she's in a short denim skirt. I swear if she bends over, I'll get a nice show. Her pink tank is low cut, allowing the top of her breasts to be exposed. Her entire demeanor tells me she wants me, especially as she practically throws herself in my arms.

"You came!" she hollers over Lee Brice's "That Don't Sound Like You". I smile and nod.

"Let's get you a beer," Claire says as she pulls me along.

Claire brings me over to a few of her flaky friends. I say

that because they act like innocent women, who in fact live for gossip and sleeping around.

"So, Clay, I hear Ashton Carpenter is back in town," Carmen says while twirling her dark hair in her hand, looking all smug.

I don't bother with a reply, just take a sip of my beer. She'll eventually get the hint. I look around the lot and catch a glimpse of Bo, and is that Sunny? They are leaned up against a pick up and they are mighty close, too close for being just friends.

"I'll be right back."

I walk toward them, hearing Claire say something behind me, no idea what she's saying and I don't really care.

As I get closer I see Sunny giggle and touch Bo's face. She then moves away from him and hops on the tailgate of the pickup. Bo walks off in a different direction, so I continue toward Sunny. I need to talk to her anyway and tell her I'm sorry for being an ass.

"Hey, Sunny—" I stop short when I see who's she with. My breath catches in my throat.

Sitting on the tailgate next to her is Ashton. Her long blonde hair is pulled to the side and she's wearing a dress with thin straps and it looks like it falls to her knees. She's barefoot. In this moment, she's my Ashton and she's fucking beautiful.

Ashton looks at me and closes her eyes, squeezing them shut as if that will make me disappear. I laugh.

"Clay," Sunny says sternly, "I'm warnin' you now, no shit." She points at my chest.

I laugh again and put my arms up in surrender.

"I'm not here to fight. I didn't even see Ashton sittin' next to you until I walked up." It's the truth.

Sunny gives me a dirty look. "Well alright then, but I mean it. No startin' shit."

I nod and look back to Ashton. She's looking down, staring at her feet. I can tell my presence has made her uncomfortable.

Bo comes up with a few beers. He goes to hand me one with a look that says, "Don't be dick." I decline the beer and hold up my barely touched one. Suddenly I don't feel like drinking. The realization occurs to me that I fucked up bad, I'm not a dick. I need to fix this shit.

"Ya'll mind if I talk to Ashton a minute?"

Bo and Sunny both turn their heads fast in my direction. Fuck.

"I just want to apologize for my behavior."

My statement causes Ashton to pop her head up and look at me. When our eyes meet, I swear I see something there. I just can't place my finger on it.

Sunny looks at Ashton. "You okay with that, Ash?"

Ashton stares, squinting at me a second longer before speaking to Sunny and Bo.

"I think I'm good, guys, give us a few." She doesn't smile, if anything she looks sad.

"Fine." Sunny jabs a finger in my chest. She is lucky I allow it. I watch as She and Bo walk off a short distance but keep their eyes on us. Whatever.

I move to stand a little closer to Ashton, not too close though. I stay standing by the side of the truck, leaning on it with my arms hanging over the bed.

Ashton says nothing, just stares out at the fields that reach the mountains. I take a few minutes to study her. Her legs are dangling over the tailgate, swinging. It reminds me of simpler times. She really hasn't changed at all. Her hair is still the same length or at least I think it is. I catch her shiver slightly. I'm not sure why she doesn't have a sweater or light jacket. Does she not remember summer nights can hit the low seventies?

"Cold?" I ask, figuring it's a great way to break the silence that is hanging between us.

Ashton glances at me. "A little. I forgot the summer evenings could be chilly. I guess being in Florida does that to you." She shrugs her shoulders, but I watch her shiver again. I would be a complete asshole if I didn't offer my flannel to her. I'm not sure she'll take it, but I decide to offer anyhow.

I shrug out of it. "Would you like this?" I hold out the red and brown checkered print flannel and wait.

I watch as Ashton opens her mouth to speak then shuts it before finally speaking. I think I've caught her off guard.

"Um… yeah, sure, thanks." She reaches out and takes it, putting it on right away. I notice her inhale and close her eyes.

For some reason that stirs something inside of me and I try my best to ignore it. I need to just say my peace and get out of here.

"Look." I pause, "I didn't mean to air our business."

She says nothing, just continues looking out in the darkness that has now taken over the sky. The bonfire has been lit and the glow coming from it hits her face just right. She looks both haunting, and I hate to admit it, sexy. What the hell am I saying? I shake my head. *Focus.*

"What I'm tryin' to say is I'm sorry for being a jerk."

Ashton finally looks at me. "I forgive you, Clay. Lord knows I ain't made the best of choices; we all mess up sometimes."

I let what she says sink in. She kind of just admitted she has fucked up some. I'll take it.

The wind blows, causing Ashton's hair to blow in my direction. I get a whiff of her and suck in my breath. She smells like fresh flowers maybe, hell I don't even know, but it smells so fucking good. It causes my dick to twitch slightly.

Nope, that's not good. I got to get away from her.

"Okay, we're okay then?" I need confirmation so I can leave.

She doesn't smile, just sighs. "I forgive you for lashing out, Clay. I deserved it, so you deserve to be forgiven. I just don't know if we'll ever be okay again. We have lots of—"

She's suddenly interrupted by Claire. "There you are, hot stuff!"

Claire grabs my ass, shocking me. Ashton grimaces and looks away quickly. She is totally reading into Claire and I. Before I can say anything, Claire opens her damn mouth.

"What are you doin' talkin' to her for?" She tugs my arm off the truck. "Come on, babe, let's go. I got somethin' waiting for you." She winks at me.

Babe? I'm certainly not her babe. No one has that claim. I'm gonna have to address that shit. I know what she's trying to pull. She's trying to lay claim on me to piss Ashton off.

"Um, Claire—"

This time Ashton cuts me off. "She's right, ya'll have a good night." She hops off the tailgate and walks away, leaving her sandals behind. I inhale her scent once more as the breeze blows. It's intoxicating and leaves me paralyzed in my spot until it fades away, leaving me feeling empty.

18

Ashton

Walking, I force myself not to look back at the two of them. It's obvious Claire has her claws into Clay. She's a modern day mean girl. I'd be lying if it didn't hurt to see her touching him and calling him pet names. I try to remind myself that Clay hasn't been mine in a long time and it shouldn't upset me that he has moved on, yet it makes me feel things I haven't in quite some time. Not to mention he could do way better than Claire. Ugh, I need to stop. Where did Sunny and Bo go off too?

It doesn't take me long to find them near the bonfire. They're laughing together and look so happy as the glow from the fire hits their faces. I decide it's better to leave them be and not interrupt. I'm not entirely sure what's happening between them, but make a mental note to ask Sunny later. I glance around once more before heading out to the road where I'm parked.

Stepping on a rock, I realize I left my sandals behind. Oh well, I'm not taking the chance on going back for them and seeing Claire and Clay.

I'm almost to my SUV when I catch a glimpse of something moving off to the side of the road. I focus my eyes for a moment to make sure it's not someone or something about to attack me and wish I never had.

There's Clay leaned up against a truck and Claire on her knees. I can't see what she's doing, but I sure can guess what's happening. My emotions get the best of me and I try to push down a sob, but it escapes me anyway. It's loud and causes Clay to turn my way. His eyes go wide when they find me. Shit.

He stands up straight and practically pushes Claire away, but the damage is done. I take off running for my truck with Clay hollering behind me. I pray he doesn't follow.

When I get to my car, I hop in right away and lock the doors. I take a deep breath then high tail it out of there before anymore shit can happen tonight.

I've calmed down by the time I reach home. I notice Aunt Lynne is sitting in her rocker, wine glass in hand. I make sure to wipe my eyes and smile before getting out. Whatever happened back there, I'm leaving back there, plus I don't want my aunt prying.

"Hey there," I say as I walk up the steps and sit down on the swing at the end of the porch. It's always been my favorite spot out here. I'd sit on this swing for hours, reading, gossiping with Sunny, and occasionally making out with Clay. Seriously, I need to remove him from my thoughts.

"Did you have a nice time out?" my aunt asks, then takes a sip of her wine. If I had to guess, I'd say it was merlot.

"It was okay, been a long time since I've been to Hillside. Not sure it's my scene these days."

"Is that so?"

"Yeah, remember people don't particularly like me. I only hung with Sunny and Bo a little and then headed out."

I watch as Aunt Lynne taps her fingers on the arm of the rocker; she's pondering something, this I know.

"I suppose that flannel was just layin' around then?" A slight smile lingers on her lips. Damn her. And damn me for being in such a rush, I forgot to give it back to Clay.

"Oh…um… no. Clay came up and noticed I was slightly cold. I forgot my cardigan."

"I see." She gets up and pulls the screen door open to go in. "I doubt that's the only thing that boy noticed about you."

She's inside before I can even think straight or come back with something. I'm baffled. I know for certain he didn't notice anything good about me. I resemble heartache, nothing more. Besides, I did just catch him getting a damn blow job.

I get up to go inside myself. I'm mentally drained. Tomorrow is another day, and unfortunately for me, I still have his damn flannel that will need to be given back. Which means I will have to see him again. I'm already dreading it, but for tonight I tell myself a lie. It's perfectly normal to curl up in bed with something that smells like Clay. All man and woodsy. Yup. Perfectly normal.

19

Ashton

I slept in Clays flannel last night. Ridiculous, I know. I just couldn't help myself. I realize I'm seriously messed up in the head. I've never once slept in Brody's clothes while he was away. That admission right there has me thinking that maybe I didn't truly love Brody. Maybe I was just desperate to move on and forget about Clay, the man currently consuming my thoughts.

I sit out, enjoying the early morning on the porch swing, coffee in hand and think back over the last couple of years and the shit choices I've made. It's the past, no going back. I've come to peace with what I did and what I can't change.

Today, I've decided it is the first day of my new life. I'm going forward and I'm going to try very hard not to look back either, except visions of Claire and Clay keeping popping up. I shake the thoughts and head inside to get ready.

After handling some work stuff and learning that I don't

need to fly back this month, I touch base with my lawyer. Glenda doesn't have good news for me. I literally sink to the floor as she deals me my shitty cards.

Brody has no fucking money left. He apparently has or had a gambling problem. That shouldn't be a shocker, he did work in the casino industry. Of course, he never mentioned that he liked to gamble to me.

With this news, I'm most likely out ten thousand dollars. Which sucks. I need that money. I sigh as I head straight to The Neon Moon. I need to talk to Bo about more hours. Working remotely has its perks and I'm thankful for the option, however it also comes with a pay cut. I wasn't too concerned about it at the time because I was planning on getting my money from Brody. *Silly Ashton, should have known better.*

Bo's at the bar with his back to me when I walk in. I waste no time; desperate times call for desperate measures.

"Hey Bo, morning,"

"Oh, hey there, wasn't expecting you today."

"I know. Look, I need more hours. Give me some night and weekends… please." I sound pathetic, but I don't even care.

"Um… you sure you want that?"

"Yes!" I say immediately, "I freaking need this, Bo, please. Brody spent all our money, my money." I take a deep breath and try hard not to burst into tears.

Bo curses under his breath. "Well shit, Ash, I'll give you more hours, but I gotta warn ya. Clay comes in often and some-times he's not alone. You gonna be good with that?"

Warning bells go off in my head at the thoughts of Clay with different women. I silence them quickly.

"I'm good, trust me, I'm good." I smile despite that nagging feeling in the back of my mind. "I've come to peace with my past and I'm looking forward. "

"Ah, that's good to hear, Ashton. I'm glad you are turning a new leaf. I've missed you."

"I'm really sorry if I've hurt you." I mean it. Bo was a great friend, I never meant to hurt him.

He comes around the side of the bar and pulls me in for a hug. Some of the tension I'm feeling leaves my body.

"Okay, how about tomorrow night?"

I pull back and look at Bo. I can't help but smile so big. That is until Clay walks in. The look on his face tells me he's not happy.

2 0

Clay

What in the fuck did I just walk in on? Bo and Ashton are hugging pretty damn close, but what really has me seeing red is the moment she leans up on her tippy toes and kisses his cheek. I all but lose my fucking shit.

"Am I interrupting something?" I don't even try to hide the anger in my voice.

"Dude… what?" Bo sounds a little panicked.

I'm not buying it. "You sure? It looked like I just walked in on you two gettin' cozy." Fuck, I don't know why I'm letting this shit get to me. It's not like Claire wasn't just sucking my dick last night, that was until Ashton walked past and everything went to hell.

Ashton starts laughing. I'm not sure what she finds funny about this, but now is not the time.

"Can I help you?" I quip at her.

"Clay," Bo starts, but Ashton lays her hand on his chest.

"It's fine Bo. I need to talk to Clay too. Thank you again, so much. I owe ya one." She pats him one last time before walking toward me. Why is she thanking him and what does she owe him? These questions are irking the shit out me, even though I have no right to care. I shouldn't care.

"Clay, can we talk? Outside maybe?" Ashton looks me up and down. I'm partially in uniform. But unless you know I'm an officer, you wouldn't think much of my attire. I'm in a solid black fitted shirt and hunter green cargos with my black work boots. I thought I would pop in before I start my shift, but now I'm second guessing whether or not that was a good idea.

I wave my hand for her to lead the way. She walks until we are just outside the bar. Ashton looks at me, her bright blue eyes holding secrets, this I know. Something passes over her face as she looks me up and down. What the hell was that? I nod my head for her to get on with it. I really don't have all day.

"Look, I just wanted to tell you I'm so sorry. For every-thing. The past, leaving you. I'm sorry." I continue staring into her eyes. I see the remorse there, but I'm not ready to forgive her.

"I got over you a long time ago, its fine." I might be slightly lying but she doesn't need to know that. I refuse to give her the satisfaction.

"Yeah… um… it's clear that you did. You and Claire last night, remember?"

So she thinks Claire and I are a thing? I scratch my chin. What about her and Bo?

"Okay, so what about you and Bo? You a thing now?" I try to keep my voice calm but it's damn hard.

"What? Where would you get that idea?"

Is she really asking me that? "I did just walk in on you both a few minutes ago." I hike my thumb back toward the bar. She can't be this damn stupid.

Ashton's laughing again, full on laughing. I haven't seen her laugh this hard in well… since forever.

"What's so funny?" I ask, confused by her reaction.

Her laughs slow before she looks at me and shakes her head, her blond hair falling in her face. I itch to reach out and swipe it away.

"Really, Clay? You're gonna sit here and question me when just last night you handed me your flannel and then I find you with Claire on her knees." She lets out a sarcastic laugh. "Don't dare question my personal life. It's none of your business anymore." Ashton storms off toward what I'm guessing is her white vehicle, some dumb crossover SUV.

Fuck this, I don't have time to deal with her shit. I turn and walk back into the bar for a minute. I call Bo's name and wait for him to appear.

He comes out with a smirk on his face. Asshole.

"Don't you dare touch her. You understand?" The words come out of my mouth before I have time to think. She's not mine. I have no right, but do it anyway.

"Dude, you are wrong on so many levels. I don't want Ashton. What you walked in on, wasn't what it looked like."

I tilt my head narrowing my eyes, "Care to explain then?"

"Look, it's really not my place—"

"Spill it, Bo." I point a finger at him.

"Fine." He huffs. "Ashton came by to apologize for the past and to ask for more hours. Her ex-husband blew all their money so she needs to pick up shifts."

I run my hands through my hair. What kind of piece of shit did she marry? I instantly feel bad for accusing them both.

"Sorry, man," I say as I turn and take off for my truck; maybe I can catch her before she gets home.

———

I had no luck driving the roads to her aunt's and had ran out of time. Now that my shift is over and it's nearly ten pm, I dare drive by her aunt's street. I can't see the house from the road and have been sitting at the end debating on just driving on up and knocking on the damn door. I'm sure Lynne would give me a damn earful for how late it is and then let it slide because she wants nothing more than for us to be together.

Just as I decide against going up the drive, a vehicle comes down the path. A white SUV. It's Ashton. Against my better judgement, I follow her.

Ashton doesn't get out of car. I probably have her to scared to get out, so I hop on out of my work truck and go up to her.

She's staring at me, clearly relieved that it is me and not some stalker. I step back, allowing her to get out of her car.

"Clay! Jesus, you scared me!" She swats me.

"I didn't mean to, I just wanted to come by and I guess apologize for my accusation this morning." Sticking my hands in my pocket, I take another step back. See, I'm not a complete ass.

"As you should." I'm glad to see she still has that smart mouth.

"Listen, I feel bad about it. I made Bo tell me what was going on between you two. I know it wasn't my place, but I had to know."

She just stands there looking at the ground.

"Ashton, look at me."

I'm not expecting the reaction from her when she does finally look at me. She looks me up and down, taking in my uniform. I watch as her eyes glisten and her mouth drops open.

"You're a cop?" An unreadable expression comes across her face, one I don't know.

"Ranch and Grove officer, but yeah."

"Oh my God," she whispers as she covers her mouth,

clearly shocked by this news. I'm not sure how she wouldn't know this. Maybe her aunt and Sunny never mentioned it. How strange?

"What are you running from the law?" I try to joke, but fall short when she starts to cry.

"Um, Ashton, are you alright?"

I realize this was probably a bad idea going out of my way to apologize. I rub my hands down my face in frustration. When she still doesn't respond, I take that as my cue to leave.

"I think it's best I go." I take a step backwards toward my truck.

As I pull open the door and hop on the running board, Ashton speaks.

"That's why I left." Her voice is so low, I think I might have misheard her.

"You what?"

Ashton points at the truck and me. "I left so you could pursue your dream."

What is she talking about? I never talked about this dream to her, but before I can question it, she has taken off up the steps to the house, leaving me more confused than ever.

21

Ashton

I can't believe it. Clay pursued his dream. I run straight into the house, straight for the bathroom, where I lock myself inside of it. Sliding down the door, I allow myself to cry.

After a few minutes I try to calm down and hope that Aunt Lynne doesn't come knocking. I was so overcome with emotion seeing him standing there in his uniform that fit him perfectly, and holy hell, did he look hot. I just couldn't stand there a minute longer. It was too much. I had set Clay free so he could follow his dreams and he followed them. In turn though, I gave up so much, so much more. I should be happy that he pursued his goal and became an officer, yet all I feel is sadness.

I start the shower and turn it all the way to hot. I need to have a good cry to wash it all away.

———

7 years prior

I came out from the apple trees, making my way to Clay's. We were going to meet some friends at Hillside for an end of senior year bonfire and s'mores night.

I walked up the porch steps to Clay's family home. It was an old farmhouse that's been renovated. Now white with black trim, it gave off a modern appearance. Pots of flowers lined the steps up to the door, giving it a welcome home feeling.

I halted though, dead in my tracks, when I heard my name come out of Clay's mouth through the opened windows. The Williams' front door was also propped open, a pot of flowers holding it in place.

I stood to the side and listened to the conversation. Clay continued talking and it left me feeling uneasy, the same feeling I got when my mama left. I held my breath and waited.

"We just want you to follow your goals, baby," Clay's mom, Susan, quietly said.

"I know ya do, Ma, but the academy is hundreds of miles away and I won't leave Ashton."

Goals? I was confused we'd always talked about staying here after graduation and attending the local college together.

"We know you do, Clay, but you have to think about your future too. Are you just going to give it all up for some girl?" Susan continued.

I'm just some girl? My heart sank. Clay had mentioned wanting to be an officer on and off over the years. I felt foolish for not listening a little more, I just assumed he would work the farm.

"She's not some girl, Ma, and you know it." Clay trailed off, but I was no longer listening.

I slowly took a step back down the steps, hoping no one saw me. I felt clammy and my mama's letter came to mind immediately. Her words kept repeating over and over in my head. I was holding Clay back. That's not what I wanted. That's not who I am. I loved Clay with all my soul. My mom left me and my dad because she claimed we held her back, and I refused to do that to Clay.

Once down the last step, I took off toward the fields. It didn't take me long to reach the trees and get lost in them.

My mind was on overdrive. I couldn't be responsible for holding Clay back. I had lived a life where my mama wasn't present. It wasn't a feeling I wanted to live with. The harsh pill of reality slowly sank down into the pit of my stomach. I knew what I needed to do even if it gutted Clay like a fish. Hell, it was to gut me wide open too. Still, it's what had to be done.

As I felt the contents in my stomach threatening to come up, I squatted and put my head between my legs. My entire world had just been turned upside down. This couldn't be real.

My cell ringing from my back pocket pulled me from my thoughts, reminding me that it was in fact real. Clay's name appeared on the screen. Shit. I didn't even want to answer, yet I had to.

"Hey," I said, praying I sounded normal.

"Where are you? You were supposed to be here by now." His words held nothing but worry and concern, which made me feel bad.

"Sorry, I got held up. I'm walkin' through the grove now."

"Oh, alright then, I'll come meet ya."

We ended the call and I knew I had three minutes tops to get my emotions in check. It was time to put on a smile and pretend I wasn't dying inside.

22

Ashton

Sunny and I sit out back in our bikinis, on a blanket soaking up the summer sun. We have some George Strait playing in the background on a boom box I dug out of Aunt Lynne's garage.

Coming from Florida, I had an abundance of swimwear. I'm currently wearing a teal and white polka dot bikini. It's one of my favorites. Sunny went through my stash over and over until she finally settled on a burgundy one that looks great on her tanned skin. It feels so good to have her by my side again. I've missed this, us and our friendship. I prop up and turn toward her.

"You know, I'm really sorry about leavin' ya when I did. It wasn't right how I went about it."

"I second that, but what I want to know is why? Why did you up and leave?"

I swallow. I don't know if I'm ready to say my reason for

leaving. I'll never be ready. However, seeing Clay last night in his work uniform, next to his truck, somehow makes it okay to finally talk about it.

"Come on, Ash, it's me. You know you can tell me anything." Sunny looks at me with a smile; it's genuine too. Her light brown hair blows in the breeze. She looks exactly the same as during our teen years, reminding me that I used to be able to tell my best friend everything.

Here goes nothing. "Just before graduation, I was walkin' up to Clay's house. His mama had the windows open, I could hear them discussing something. I know, I know, it's rude to eavesdrop, but I heard my name." I have to pause for a minute, I don't know why it's so hard to talk about this after all these years. I take a deep breath as I pick at some grass. I need to talk about this, to let it out.

Sunny reaches over a squeezes my hand. "Go on, Ash."

I look down at our hands and suddenly know it'll be okay to share this secret with her.

"I heard them talking about Clay going to the police academy. His mama said I was gonna hold him back. I couldn't do that, Sunny. My mama left me and my daddy because we held her back from her dreams. I couldn't go through that again. I had to leave so he would go make something of himself. And look--he did." I choke up at the last bit.

"Oh, Ashton!" Sunny pulls me to her and hugs me, holding me for a minute.

I'm the first to pull away, having to wipe my eyes. "I'm sorry I never told you. I didn't know how to face the reality of it and as time went on. I just wanted to forget it all."

"Look at me, Ash, you did what you knew to be best at eighteen. You got dealt a shit hand with your mama runnin' off. You didn't have anyone to go to about these things."

"I know, you know, I do. It's just I felt terrible and lost myself in the process."

"Hey now, you didn't lose yourself entirely. You're makin' a comeback." Sunny nudges me with her arm to make me feel better. It does for the most part, yet something is still eating away at me. I close my eyes briefly and turn my face up to the sky, allowing the sun to warm my face.

"Will you promise me one thing?" I ask looking back to Sunny, I need this confirmation from her.

"Sure." She holds up her pinky. Pinky promises were a thing of our past, it's nice to know she hasn't forgotten.

"You can't tell anyone. I want to be able to tell Clay myself. I don't want him hearing it from no one else."

Sunny smiles a giant smile. "Promise. So you gonna tell him?"

"Yes, it's just a matter of when. Our last few encounters haven't been the best, so I want to make sure the timing is right."

"Good, as long as you tell him. He needs to know." She pauses before squeezing my hand again. "He's harboring some deep stuff too. It all needs to be set free."

I feel what she is saying, right down to my core. He deserves to know so we can both be set free.

23

Ashton

Fourth of July weekend is here and Sunny insists on going down to The Neon Moon on my only night off. I groan as I read over the text message from her again.

Be ready by 8pm.

I send a quick reply back hoping she drops it.

I have nothing to wear.

Not even a minute later she responds:

I got you somethin'

Of course she did. Damn her. That leaves me no choice but to go.

Fine, but I'm not staying out all night.

I toss my phone on the bed, leaving it behind so I can have a little peace and quiet before later. For now, I'm going to sit on the front porch and read some Abbi Glines.

———

"Are you sure about this?" I say as Sunny pulls into a spot. It's packed and we had to drive around a bit to find a place to park.

"Totally, we are gonna have a blast!"

I'm glad one of us is excited about this. I'm dreading it. I haven't run into Clay in over two weeks. Work has been good, no one threw daggers my way, and I have been on the up about living back here. Tonight, however, is different. Chances are Clay will definitely be inside and he probably won't be alone.

I look down at my outfit that Sunny brought over. It's cute, though revealing. It's an American flag tank that ties in the front. It rests just above my belly button, exposing a little skin. It's also low cut so it shows of my chest too. The denim skirt I'm wearing is short, a good three inches above the knee. As long as I don't drop anything I should be good. I don't mind the look at all, it just puts me on display and I'm not exactly looking to call attraction to myself. Sunny, however, insisted. She told me to start living, and well, here I am.

We walk in and find Madi working the bar. Bo is on the other side, talking with people who look familiar but I can't place.

"Bo!" Sunny hollers and throws her arms around him. Yup, I need to ask her about that later.

"Hey, guys. Ashton, you remember Blue?" Bo points to Blue and that's when it clicks on who's who.

"Yeah. Hey." I give a small wave and keep my distance.

"This is my girlfriend, Tabby," Blue says. It's obvious they are together by the way they look at each other. They are adorable and it makes me slightly jealous.

It's not long before we grab beers and wonder over the small dance floor. There's a DJ here tonight playing a mix of upbeat pop stuff and some country. I love the mix up.

Sunny and I finish up dancing our tails off to some Usher and decide to get another drink. As we're walking up to the bar, I spot him. His back is to me. His brown hair is covered by a trucker's hat tonight; even so, I know it's him. I know it's him just by the way he stands, straight, tall, and confident. He turns our way just as we get to the bar.

"Ladies," Clay tips his hat slightly and goes back to his beer. Okay, that didn't go so bad. Madi hands us our beers and we turn to go but run right into Claire and her entourage. Claire gives me the stare down. Why, I don't even know.

"Excuse me," I politely say as I try to make my way around them.

"That's right, go away. No one wants you here, Ashton." Claire's words slice through the air and her dumb friends snicker behind her.

"Um, I'm not sure what you're getting at, but I'm not here for no one so that shouldn't be a problem." I throw my hair over my shoulder for good measure. I'd decided to leave it straight tonight. Curling it took to much effort.

Her and her friends gasp, and I believe I heard Clay snort but can't be certain. I walk past them just as Claire steps in front of me again.

"You look like a slut. It won't make him want you. He is with me now so stay away."

I study Claire for a second. Her blonde hair could use a trim, and I'd say if she didn't have such an ugly personality, she would be beautiful. Such a waste of beauty.

I throw my hands on my hips before telling her where to go.

"Claire, hun, I look like me. For the first time in a long time, I look like myself. If that makes me look like a slut, then so be it. I won't be losing sleep over it. Perhaps you shouldn't worry so much about what I look like and focus more on yourself." I pause, smiling my biggest smile. "As far as he goes," I use air quotes, "you can have him. I already had him."

With that, I walk off with my beer in hand, Sunny coming up next to me laughing hard.

"That was epic, Ash! You should have seen her face!" Sunny's still dying laughing as we start dancing to some song I don't recognize. It has a great beat so I go a long with it.

Two songs later, Sunny declares she's going to get us more beer. I'm enjoying the music so I wave her off and continue dancing. I feel someone grab my wrist only to turn and see Clay standing there. I stop dancing right away.

"Is everything okay?" I look beyond him to look for Sunny or Claire, but I can't see either so I look back to him. What's going on?

"Everything is fine. Ashton, I want to talk."

"Right now?" He wants to talk now? "Can't we do this another day?"

Just then a slow country song comes on, "Didn't You Know How Much I Loved You" by Kellie Picker. Clay grabs my hands.

"Dance with me."

I say nothing, just nod cautiously and look again for Sunny. He doesn't say anything either, just stares at me with his deep blue eyes. Their intense and it makes me feel things I should not be feeling. When he places his hands on my hips I feel the electricity; it runs through me. He hasn't touched me in years. His touch alone sets me afire and I'm not sure how I should feel about it.

I try to focus on the words of the song. This song is too

much. The words, the meaning, It's all too much, I'm beginning to feel every word Kellie sings. Clay's grip on my hips tells me he's feeling it too. I can't do this. Shaking my head, I pull away from him and take off.

I rush toward the entrance. I just need some air.

"Ashton," Clay calls after me, his deep voice is stern. He grabs my wrist gently and corners me against the wall. Its brick and oh so very cold, I welcome it. I need something to cool me down because Clay's touch alone has me on fire. The way he encases me outside the bar does little to ease the heat I am feeling. He's way to close to my body; he's not touching me, but he might as well be. His scent alone makes me wanna throw myself at him like a desperate child whose toy is out of reach.

"Look at me, Ashton."

I do, I look at him. And I see it, there's something smoldering in his pools of sapphire. Before I can figure out what's happening, his lips are on mine.

24

Clay

I couldn't resist. Feeling her lips on mine, they feel incredible. I snake my tongue into her mouth, getting her to open so I can deepen the kiss. The minute a moan escapes her, my dick instantly hardens. I continue kissing her while resisting the urge to remove my hands from the exterior of the bar and wrap them around her, but nope. I can't go there. The only part of us that's touching is our lips, but fuck if I don't want to be touching every inch of her right now and I don't even know why. I should hate her, it's just right in this moment she tastes too good to care about anything else.

I feel her pull back slightly so I push off the wall and take a step back. Fuck. What just happened was great, yet shitty all wrapped up in a giant explosive. What the hell am I doing? I run my hands through my hair. Looking at Ashton, I can tell she is struggling internally as well. Her brows are scrunched up and she is touching her lips with her fingers. The wind blows and I swear her scent tries to pull me back in, but I fight the urge.

We stay silent for a minute, maybe two, hell I'm not sure. It's starting to make me nervous. Ashton won't even look at me.

"Ashton… say something."

She doesn't and that makes me question if my stupid urge has now caused bigger problems than we already had.

"I don't know what came over me. I'm sorry." I blurt the words out so fast, I'm not sure if she even understood me. I take a step back to give her more space.

When she finally looks up at me, I let out a breath I didn't know I was holding. Her face is void of any emotion.

"You really shouldn't be doin' that, Clay. Claire isn't gonna like it, plus I ain't ever known you to be the kind of guy to cheat."

So that's what she's been stewing over? I laugh, a good ol' laugh. She thinks I'm with Claire.

"I don't see nothing funny about this. You can't just go around kissing women and dancing with them, not when you have a girlfriend."

Her hand has now left her lips and is on her hip. She sure looks cute when she's mad. The way her accent comes through as she is yelling is sexy. I've missed it.

She clearly doesn't need me to calm her down these days. She's come a long way. I'm actually a little upset about that. I used to be the one to calm her when a storm was brewing. I can't help but look back at her lips, the same ones I was just kissing. They are swollen. I did that to her. It causes my dick to twitch more.

"Clay Williams! What do you have to say for yourself?"

Oh, she's mad now. I kinda like it.

"I think your confused, delusional maybe." Yup, I know I'm about to set her off, yet I do it anyway.

"I'm not confused! Did you forget I saw her suckin' your cock out by the road!"

Ugh. I throw my head back. I didn't forget, I was just hoping for I don't even know… maybe to never talk about it with Ashton.

"That's what I thought. You can think what you want about me these days, but I ain't about to ruffle no feathers. You hear me. I won't be your side chick or whatever it is they call it."

"You thought wrong and have no idea what you're talkin' about." I really should clear the air about Claire and I, but I'm enjoying her go on her tirade and this is payback.

"I'm not wrong and you know it!" She thrusts a finger at my chest. I didn't imagine seeing you leaned up against some vehicle with your head thrown back. I didn't imagine Claire on her damn knees either. "What kind of man are you?"

"Drop it, Ashton." Now, I'm getting a little annoyed. After her leaving years ago, she thinks she is the one who should be angry, well, she better think again.

"No, Clay, I won't drop it. Why are all men the same?" She throws her hands in the air. "Y'all think it's okay to mess around. It's wrong and you are just like my ex, a damn cheater." Ashton shoves past me and storms off back into the bar.

How fucking dare she compare me to her fucking ex! I storm back in after her, this isn't over.

I've almost reached her when Claire steps in front of me.

"Don't you go chasin' after her. She ain't worth it."

"Not now, Claire." I side step and continue on my way. I could kick myself for messing around with her. She is an entirely different level of crazy.

Ashton is running her mouth loudly when I walk up. Sunny locks eyes with me and shakes her head to Ashton, but she keeps right on bitching.

"The nerve of him! Kissing me when he's stickin' his cock

elsewhere. I would have never thought Clay, my Clay, would become a womanizer."

Her Clay? I haven't been hers in seven long years.

That girl infuriates me to the point that I just want to stick my cock in her mouth to get her to shut up. My dick twitches in my jeans. Fuck! I shouldn't have these thoughts about her. She is everything I no longer want in my life. I shouldn't want her at all. That kiss was a mistake. My dick, though, wants her pretty little lips wrapped around it. I groan in frustration as Ashton turns to glare at me.

"Fuck this." I turn and walk away.

I go to the bar and order a beer, hoping to calm down some. I don't know why I let her get to me. Madi slides over my bottle and nods her head.

"What's wrong?"

"Nothing,"

"Uh huh."

I sigh. "It's Ashton."

"I figured. I don't know, ya might want to do something about all the sexual tension you're harboring for her." She winks and walks down the bar to tend to someone else.

Sexual tension… maybe. I haven't been able to sleep with anyone since Ashton came back and I laid eyes on her. I tried with Claire, but even her sucking my dick wasn't working for me. All I kept thinking about was that gorgeous blonde with the blue eyes who stole my heart. I take a swig of my beer, feeling some of my anger deflate. It dawns on me that maybe we are playing a game of cat and mouse. I slide off the stool and head back over to Ashton.

She's sitting in a booth with Sunny, laughing about something. With the lights dimmed, she looks so carefree that I almost think twice about what I'm about to do. However, when she glances my way and does a double take, I see it. There's fury in her eyes, laced with desire maybe. At least that's what I tell myself it is. Yup. Desire.

This could go one of two ways: she slaps me across the face or she comes with me. I walk straight up and pull her out of the booth, kissing her hard. She goes still in my arms but it doesn't take long for her to melt into me.

Meanwhile, everyone around us starts hollering, and I know it's it regards to us. Ashton pulls away quickly. I don't think so. I reach for her wrist and pull her back into me, whispering in her ear.

"Come with me."

I feel her head shake no. I know she's uncertain because of what happened outside.

"Claire isn't my girlfriend, now come with me." I hear the intake of her breath and hope like hell she will just come with me so we can get this over with. If I can get her out of my system, we'll both be better off.

I pull back slightly to make eye contact with her; she's biting her lip, and damn if it isn't sexy. My dick straining against my jeans tells me it's now or never with her so I tug her toward me.

Ashton turns to look at Sunny and I follow suit. She is staring us dead, mouth dropped open. I wink at her.

"Come on, Ashton."

"Where are we gonna go?"

"You'll see," I say as I smile at her.

It does the trick because she relaxes her stance and allows me to pull her through the crowd. I pay no attention to those calling after me, and I sure as hell don't miss the look Bo shoots me as the two of us walk past him and out the door.

25

Ashton

I don't know why I allowed Clay to lead me out of the bar and into his truck. He held the door open for me to climb in before going to the driver side. Once he climbs in though, it is as if the cab gets a hundred degrees hotter and I can feel my heartbeat pick up. I turn to look at Clay, who is staring back at me. I can't read his face and it doesn't really matter because the next second he leans over and puts his hand around my neck, closing in for a kiss.

Clay kissing me has never been full of such angst. I fist his hair and pull him closer to me. Right now I want nothing more than to just stay like this.

Sadly, he pulls away all too soon, leaving me hot and bothered. Damn, it's been a long time since I've been this turned on.

"I need to get you home," he says as he adjusts himself and turns on the truck. I smile, knowing I'm the cause of his erection.

"I know you are sittin' over there with a smirk. Just wait."

I pull my lip in between my teeth; nerves are starting to kick in. I haven't been with anyone since Brody and well, it's been months. Not to mention our sex life wasn't something to brag about. If I'm being honest, sex with Brody was something I dreaded. He didn't care about anything except getting off. There was no intimacy, no pleasuring me. Nope. He was all about him.

The drive to Clay's is quiet. The air filled with electricity. I've only ever felt that electricity with Clay and the last time I felt it, was the night I gave myself to him.

I sigh thinking back. I was so young and thought I was doing what was right. If I've learned anything since returning home, it's that you can't go back and change the past, you just gotta keep moving forward and hope for a better tomorrow. Is this what we're doing? Moving forward? Doubtful, we have too much history. This will most likely end badly, yet I'm still going along with this, whatever it is.

We pull down a dark narrow road that looks more like a driveway. I don't ever remember this road, so perhaps it's the path to his place.

We come to a stop in front of a garage that's separated from a brick house. It's not too big, but looks cozy from the outside. Is this where Clay lives? A tinge of guilt hits me and I can't help but wonder if this would have been our first home together.

Clay cutting the engine snaps me out of it and suddenly I feel nervous. What am I even doing right now? I stare straight ahead, afraid to even make eye contact with him.

I hear him get out of the truck and watch him round the front of the truck, coming for me. As he opens the door I panic and scoot toward the middle seat. He looks at me with a questioning look.

"Are you okay, Ashton?"

"What are we doing? Is this your house?" I vomit the questions out fast. I can't help it.

Clay laughs slightly. "To answer your questions, I'm not sure what we are doing or what will happen. I just know that I want you in my bed. Also, yes, this is my house."

Clays eyes never leave mine; he's blunt, yet honest. I nod my head, still unsure about all of this.

When I don't move, Clay climbs on the running board and leans in the cab. I watch as his eyes roam over me, stopping at my mini skirt. I shift, my legs are parted slightly due to how I'm sitting in his truck. His eyes come back to me and I see the heat in them. Is it possible for them to darken more than they already are?

His hand follows up my left leg until he hits my inner thigh. The goosebumps that crawl over me are begging for more, while leaving little trails of heat in their wake.

His hand inches closer up my thigh, stopping just before my panties, leaving me anxious.

"Can I?"

That's why he stopped, he's asking permission.

"Ashton, I won't touch you unless you tell me to." He smirks and brings his fingers back down toward my knee. Damn him for teasing me.

I go to nod my head just as he removes his hand. He grabs my hips quickly, causing me to yelp as he slides me closer to him.

He doesn't release my hips and I feel a little exposed. I'm sure he's getting a view up my skirt.

Clay leans into me; he's so close I can see the vein in his neck is popping in excitement. I can guarantee my vein looks identical.

"I'm gonna ask again." He pauses to pull back and look at

me. "This time I want an answer. Can I touch you?" His voice is rough with need. I want this just a badly as he does; even if giving in is a bad idea, I'm going to do it anyway.

"Yes."

"Yes, what?"

He's going to make me spell it out for him. That ass, I've never asked or begged to be touched, however, this is turning me on more than I'd care to admit.

"Yes, Clay… you can touch me."

The minute the words leave my mouth, his right hand leaves my hip and trails my inner thigh again. I close my eyes in anticipation of what's next. Clay rubs a finger over my panties and then pulls them aside. His fingers just rest on me, not moving. It's straight agony. I open my eyes to see what the hold up is.

Clay is staring at me through hooded eyes; they're intense and I can see the war waging in them.

"What's wrong?" I go to scoot back some, but his other hand still has a grip on me and he tightens it, refusing to let me move.

"I want you to look at me, Ashton. Do not close your eyes." His voice is strained with need.

"Um... okay…"

Just please fucking touch me already. I don't say that bit out loud, seriously just touch me. I need to feel his hands on me again.

The minute his finger runs up and down my slick fold, I throw my head back, letting out a moan.

"Look at me," Clay commands as he continues running his finger up and down.

I look back to him. This might be the most intimate thing I've ever done, aside from losing my virginity to him.

Clay dips a finger inside of me and it takes all my will power to not close my eyes. He thrust it in and out a few times before adding a second finger, stretching me. God, this feels so good.

"So wet for me," he growls, still never taking his eyes off of me.

I say nothing, it's obvious that he makes me wet with need.

He speeds up his thrusts, causing me to nearly buck off the seat. His touch has me losing all train of thought as I let a moan escape me. Without thinking, I close my eyes, which is a mistake.

Clay stops moving and pulls his fingers out of me, leaving me feeling empty. He brings his fingers to his lips and sucks them one by one. Holy hell! I'm not sure if I should be embarrassed or more turned on. I squeeze my legs together and turn away from his eyes, but he pushes them back apart.

"You taste so fucking good, and don't you dare get shy on me now."

It's like he can read my mind. Then again, Clay and I used to know each other better than we knew ourselves, I shouldn't be surprised that he can read me.

He pulls me to the very edge, so close that I feel like I'm going to fall right out on my ass if he lets go of my legs.

"Clay, what are you doing?!"

He shifts between my legs, throwing each one over his shoulders. His arms are bigger that I remember, more defined.

"Do you trust me?"

"I... well, I don't really know." It's not exactly a lie.

He crouches down a little and brings both hands up my skirt and in one swift move, he tears my panties right off of me. The swift motion causes me to shriek out.

Since when did he learn how do such things? He leaves me no time to dwell on it because in the next minute he's pushing my skirt up above my ass and brings his mouth to where my panties just were. He snakes his tongue out, causing me to buck again.

HOLY FUCKING SHIT!

He licks forcefully while sucking gently. The flicks of his tongue against me feels so good. In fact, I don't think I've ever felt this good. I fist my hands in his hair, keeping him in place.

It's not long before I feel myself threatening to break free. I need more. Right now.

"Clay! More… please!"

He does as I ask. He picks up the pace, sucking harder, flicking faster. That's when I come undone. Legs shaking around his face as ripples of pure ecstasy rip through me. I'm left feeling out of breath, too tired to even care that I'm on the edge of the seat of the seat and could fall at any second. Thankfully he is still holding on, preventing me from falling out.

It's unlike anything I've ever done or experienced before and now that I've had a taste, I'm afraid I'll want more, and Clay's mouth is a dangerous thing to want.

26

Clay

I know for certain two things. One, Ashton tastes like heaven and I want, no scratch that, I need to taste more of her. Two, I need to get her inside the house NOW before I take her right here. Feeling her come apart in my mouth was everything I dreamed it would be, I had always imagined what she would taste like. Teenage Clay would be proud.

I slowly move her legs, while continuing to hold her so she doesn't fall. Lifting her off the seat, I pull her skirt back down. I take her hand in mine and help her down out of the truck.

"Come on," I tell her.

I don't remove my hand from hers. Part of me fears she'll turn around and run. I'm not risking it.

Ashton says nothing as I unlock the door and allow her to walk in first. I watch as she takes in her surroundings. I only bring chicks back to this house. This is not my home. I shake my head as I mentally remind myself of the fact.

"Your house is… simple." She turns to look at me.

I shrug my shoulders. "It's a house." The less we talk about this, the better. I lead her down the hall to the room.

Once in the room, I don't call it my room, because well it's not. I dim the lights a little. Setting the mood is important, but I still want to be able to see all of Ashton.

"Take off your clothes," I command.

"What?! I don't know about this, Clay."

Ashton wrings her fingers in front of her and looks down. She almost looks innocent. In some ways, maybe she is. Maybe she isn't. I've missed years of Ashton and have no idea what to expect now. I'm sick of waiting to find out though.

"Clothes off now." I step away from her giving her space.

She peeks up at me through her long lashes, her cheeks flushed.

"If you want this," I point back and forth between us, "you'll have to lose your clothes."

I mean it, I'm not about to take advantage. As much as I want to rip that short ass skirt off of her along with her skimpy top, I won't do it. That's not how I do things.

"It's just… I'm not experienced in all this." Ashton trails off, refusing to look at me. Is it possible that she looks more flustered than before?

"Not experienced? I'm not sure I'm following."

I wait, unsure of what she means. She lets out a breath as she pulls some of her hair over her shoulder and starts twisting it in her hand.

"Clay, I have only been with you and Brody. I'm not innocent by any means, it's just sex hasn't really been exciting. I'm not sure I'm what you want."

Is she kidding? Not want I want? I have wanted this woman since we were kids and while I should hate her, I can't seem to right this moment. I'm sick of fighting it, this desire to have her.

I walk over to her in two strides and cup her chin, tilting it so she has to look at me.

"Ashton, never worry about what I want. I know exactly what I want."

She says nothing in return, just nods and smiles shyly. She takes a step back and takes off her boots. I watch in anticipation. Next goes her skirt, exposing her bare. I had forgotten that I ripped her panties off in the truck. She slowly slides the skirt down her tan, toned legs. I can't help but picture them back around me. My dick strains at the thought and I have to adjust myself in my jeans. I need to lose them ASAP. Especially after watching her pull the tank over her head. Her stomach is toned too, tits are about to pop right out of the barely there, red, lace bra.

Holy. Fucking. Shit.

Ashton is perfect.

Ashton is beautiful.

I want her now more than I ever have before. I didn't think it was possible to want someone so bad, until right now as she stands in front of me, wearing nothing but a red bra. Fuck, I am in way over my head.

"You're fucking beautiful."

She smiles back, unsure of what to do with her hands. An idea comes to mind.

"Take off my clothes." Yup, I'm gluten for punishment.

She takes a nervous step toward me and I can't help but smile. I love seeing her like this.

I kick my boots off as she starts unbuttoning my shirt. I want her to hurry it up because I really can't wait to bury my dick inside her, but at the same time I want to savor every second of this.

As she lets my shirt fall to the floor, my breathing picks up slightly. She'll see my tattoo on my chest and will know exactly what it means.

It's two apple trees wrapped around each other. They've clashed together to form one.

I watch her study it with her eyes before a shaky hand traces it. We haven't been intimate like this in a very long time and it stirs something in me. I reach out and rub my thumb across her lips. She looks at me with those piercing blue eyes.

"Clay," she whispers before her lips descend on mine. There's so much force in her kiss, I have to take a step back to ground us. I need to have her now. As much as I don't want to break the kiss, I do.

"Finish undressing me, Ashton, now"

"Okay, Mr. Bossy."

I smile, there's the girl I use to know. Feisty and sexy all rolled into one.

The minute her hands move to my jeans, I link my hands behind my head. This has to be all her. I want her to want this just as much as I do, she needs to prove that to me.

When she springs my cock free from my briefs I see her expression change. I almost think she's going to back out of what we're about to do until she reaches up and strokes me. I throw my head back and curse. Her soft hands tremble ever so slightly as she runs her hand up and down. It takes sheer willpower to not blow my shit right then and there. I need her to stop now or the show is going to end before it even gets started.

I grab her wrist, and she snaps her eyes up to me.

"Get on the bed."

She wastes no time at all going over to my king size bed. Its covered by a black comforter and sheets. No fancy ass pillows.

Ashton climbs to the center of the bed while I make a mental note to have her bent over, ass up for me in the near future. Not tonight though, I want her complete attention and I want her eyes on me the entire time.

I reach into the nightstand grabbing a condom before I climb on the bed to join her.

She looks at the condom and smiles.

"Good idea."

"I'm no dummy".

"Never said you were." She winks at me playfully.

I spread her thighs apart and press a finger inside of her still wet folds. I watch her the entire time I thrust my fingers in and out, moving them around to stretch her. Her head is back, eyes closed. It's surreal to see her like this.

When I start to feel her tighten, I remove my fingers and make quick work of putting the condom on. She's ready, and lord knows I'm fucking beyond ready.

Ashton's breathing heavy as I settle above her, but before I enter, I make sure she's still on the same page.

"Is this what you want?"

She nods while pulling her bottom lip in her mouth. That's not good enough, I need words.

"Ashton, I need words, do you want me to fuck you now?"

"Yes." Her eyes lock on mine, telling me everything I need to know.

The minute I enter her, the whole world stills. She's so tight and it's killing me. Ashton's eyes are closed and she's breathing heavy. I can tell she is feeling the exact same.

"Look at me," I say as I pull her bra down, letting her tits pop free. I take one nipple in my mouth, nipping it gently.

"Mmm." She moans, edging me on.

I continue the assault of her nipple as I move slowly, letting her adjust to me before picking up the pace, never once taking my eyes off her. God, she feels so damn good. Better than I remember all those years ago. The intensity is a thousand times stronger. She fights hard to continue looking at me. I know what I'm doing to her is too much. It is, even for me, but I'm not stopping. I want her to feel everything I am feeling.

"You feel so good," I lean to whisper in her ear. "You're so tight for me."

My words must push her closer to the edge. I feel her tighten around me and god it feels so good. I thrust harder, Ashton meeting my movements.

"Clay! Oh my god! Don't stop!"

Ashton claws at my chest as she screams out and comes apart below me. Her words are my undoing. I grab a hold of the sheets and let go.

That night, instead of watching fireworks, we created our very own and they were far better than any show I'd ever seen. Who knew the two of us would be so explosive?

27

Ashton

That was the best sex I've ever had. Like seriously, the best. I thought I was going to combust, Clay made me feel that good.

Now here I am, laying in his arms. It feels right, listening to the beating of his heart. Dare I say it feels like home?

Being in his arms open the door to a lot of other emotions. My mind is reeling, but one thing I know for sure is that I will remember tonight. I'm burning it to my memory. The way his lips felt on mine, how his hands touched me, how he felt inside of me, I'm mentally storing it all so I never forget it. I don't want to ever forget it.

"Stop thinking and go to sleep." Clay's words cause me to lift my head so I can look at him.

"How'd ya know?"

"Because I know you." He barely whispers loud enough for me to hear him, but I do.

I sigh and lay my head back down. He deserves to know how sorry I am for the past. Maybe it's the high I'm coming down from, nevertheless he deserves closure.

"I'm sorry for leavin' you the way I did."

"Why? That's what I want to know, is why you left me."

I should tell him, but our night has been amazing and I'm not ready for it to end. I'll tell him tomorrow. Maybe.

"It's complicated. Go to sleep and I'll tell you in the morning."

"I'm holding you to that, Ashton."

Of course he will and when I tell him, I have a feeling it'll be like breaking his heart all over again.

———

I wake to the sound of knocking. At first I think I'm dreaming, but it doesn't stop. I reach for Clay and nudge him. He's still dead asleep so I climb out of bed, forgetting I'm completely naked.

After we had sex, Clay cleaned me up and took off my bra. He made me feel cherished, which is something I'm not used to.

The knocking continues as I throw my clothes back on sans bra because I can't locate it. I quietly walk out of the room and head in the direction of the knocking that won't freaking stop.

I unlock the door and pull it open. Yup, stupid I know. I haven't been known to be very smart.

On the other side of the door stands Claire. A very pissed off Claire, I might add.

"So it is true. Clay did take ya back to his fuck pad."

I'm taken aback. Clay's what?

"I'm sorry?" I stare at her with a questioning look.

"You don't know? Oh, honey, you really are a fool. This is

the house Clay brings girls to fuck. He never takes 'em to his actual home. Surely you remember the apple farm, that's where he lives." Claire laughs and it feels like I've just been slapped across the face. A terrible reminder that I am nothing special to him, despite how he made me feel last night. I'm just another girl. How many girls has he slept with? Never mind, I don't want to know. Nope. Not ever.

Claire reaches out and touches my arm as if to soothe me. I yank it back. I don't want her touching me.

"I kinda feel bad that you had to find out like this. I really thought ya knew." She winks.

What a bitch. I smirk in response. I refuse to let her see me crumble. She will not see my hurt.

"I'm totally fine, thanks for stopping by. I needed the wake up call. I forgot to set my alarm." I pause, smiling, "Well, I need to be going."

With that I quietly shut the door in her face, then turn around and burst into tears. I walk into his living room and look around. It's completely bare. Nothing personal sits on the end tables. No pictures. It looks like a stage home. There is nothing that makes this house a home. Sadness creeps over me.

I really am nothing to him. Serves me right. I broke his heart and he in turn just got his payback.

I need to get out of here and fast, before he wakes up. I tip toe back to the bedroom to retrieve my phone.

I grab my boots and phone. I still couldn't find my bra. He can keep it at this point.

Once back in the living room, I throw my boots on quickly and head straight for the door. My hands are on the knob, ready to turn it when I suddenly feel dejavu. Part of me feels bad for running out on him again, after a night of sex.

I decide to leave a note, except I can't find a notepad anywhere so I grab a napkin. It'll have to do.

Thinking quickly of what to say, I become a tad angry. This entire situation makes my skin crawl.

> *Clay-*
> *Last night was great or at least I thought it was until*
>   *Claire stood at your door this morning telling*
>   *me this was your fuck pad. I'm not a one night*
>   *stand kinda girl, but thanks for the good time.*
> *Ash*

I leave it on the table, hoping he'll find it and then I walk out of Clay's "fuck pad." Screw him.

You already did that Ashton. Ugh. I groan while rushing down his driveway.

I send a text to Sunny as I walk as fast as I can down his long driveway.

> `Leavin' Clay's. Come pick me up on the road`
> `           from his fuck pad.`

I hit send and wipe the stray tear that fell down my cheek. Shit. I send another text.

> `Hurry. I have to pee.`

With the chaos of the morning, I didn't think to use the bathroom before leaving. Ugh.

While walking to the road, all I could think about was the way his fingers touch me. The things he did with his tongue. I would have assumed that was reserved for special moments. But knowing now what I know, he must do that with all the chicks he brings there. Just the thought makes me feel dirty and ashamed. I need a hot shower so I can scrub him off of me.

Stupid girl. Such a stupid, stupid girl, Ashton.

28

Ashton

After Sunny picked me up and brought me home, I jumped straight in the shower. I turned it to the hottest it would go and then stood under the spray, letting it burn me and wash away Clay. Straight down the drain it all went, right along with my heart.

Now here I stand at The Neon Moon, working the midday shift. I'm thankful for the distraction and hope like hell he doesn't come in here looking for me.

Bo comes from out front with a list in his hand.

"Would ya mind running to the store for me? I need a few things that my supplier is out of."

"Sure thing," Now I'll have even less of a chance of seeing Clay. You betcha, I'll jump on that train.

"Thanks, you're a life saver. Here you go, call me if you have any questions."

"Will do."

I grab my stuff and set off for the local food mart two blocks away. I haven't been to Marty's Mart in years. It's funny, the place still smells exactly as I remember it. I round the corner after grabbing the produce Bo needed and run smack dab into someone, causing me to drop the lemons and limes.

"Oh my gosh, I'm so sorry!" I blurt out and look at the woman I plowed into. Shock sets in. I just ran right into Mrs. Williams, literally.

I smile at her. "Hello, Mrs. Williams." I bend down and start to gather up the fruit. When I stand back up the woman is glaring back at me, lips pressed into a thin line. Her evil stare alone nearly causes me to drop everything all over again.

"I heard you were back in town." Her tone is clipped as she brushes out her dress that I'm sure I just wrinkled.

Clay's mother continues to give me this ice cold stare. Her piercing dark blue eyes, the exact color of Clay's, look me up and down. A disgusted look etches across her face. Now I have never known his mama to be mean, but the look she is giving me now has me second guessing the woman I use to know.

"I hear you were with my son last night."

I suck in a breath and nod. How on earth does she know?

"Are you back to snake Clay in and then crush him all over again?"

"What?! What... No, I'm not—" I start stuttering but can't seem to form coherent words so I just shut up.

"I don't want you around my boy. You hear me? You are no good for him. Just like your mother. No good, you're nothing but a leaver. It's in your genes."

I gasp and take a step backwards. I feel like the wind has just been knocked out of me.

"What's wrong, pretty girl? Did I say something to upset you? Does the truth hurt?"

I just shake my head, as I'm on the verge of crying.

Mrs. Williams takes a step closer. "Let me make myself clear. Clay has a good life. Much better since you ran off. He's got a girl who wants him and will make him very happy. I don't need you gettin' in the way of that. You hear me?"

I'm confused, more secrets? A girl who wants him?

"Wh... who?" Not like it's my business, yet I ask anyway.

"Sweet Claire Matthews. I'm sure you remember her from school. She's just the sweetest and will be just what Clay needs, unlike you." She smiles a fake smile. She knows she has hit a mark with me. There's no way I can hide the anguish on my face. It's bad enough I'm fighting tears.

I try my hardest to swallow my pride and clear my throat, "Mrs. Williams, I'm not sure what you think I'm doing, but I just want Clay to be happy. That's all. I have no ill intentions."

"I'll bet you don't. You just steer clear and let him be, he doesn't need trash like you." She clicks her tongue before turning her nose up and walking away.

I exhale and look around. Fuck me, there are locals staring at me. They just watched our exchange. This will give them something to talk about for weeks. *So much for staying under the radar.* Ugh, I wish I could melt into one of the displays but that's not going to happen so instead I hold my head high and avoid eye contact with everyone as I check out.

Oh, the irony. I left the bar to avoid Clay and run right into his mama who now hates my guts. I rush back to the bar as quickly as I can in hopes of not running into anyone else in this small town.

And fuck me if I don't open the door to the bar and see Clay sitting there with a drink in front of him and a napkin in his hand. The same napkin I left for him hours before.

29

Clay

When I woke up and Ashton wasn't next to me, I was shocked. I'll admit I was mad as hell. Yet, I shouldn't be surprised, after all it's what she does best. I needed to remind myself that it was typical of her. Proof she hasn't changed. I wanted to believe maybe, just maybe she had. Despite last night and how fucking good she felt, I can't fall down that hole. Not again.

Regret starts to rear its ugly head. There's a little voice in the back of my head that keeps telling me I still love her and it needs to quiet. Ashton can't love me back, there's no point.

After throwing on some briefs I decided to go make coffee before cleaning up from last night. As much as I'd like to leave the bed smelling like her, a mix of flowers and fresh apples, I won't.

Grabbing my coffee and walking to the table, I plop down and start scrolling through my phone. Loads of texts from

Claire, I don't bother to open them. I'm not in the mood for her drama. There's a missed call and a text from my mama. I'll open hers.

<pre>
Clay I raised you better than that. Trash is
          not good company to keep.
</pre>

What the hell does that mean? Scrubbing my face with my hands, something catches my eye. A random napkin laid out. I focus on it for a few seconds and realize there's words written on it. I reach over and read it.

WHAT THE ACTUAL FUCK?

Claire was here? Fucking Claire! FUCK! I grab at my hair, my fuck pad? Seriously?! I'm livid. This can't be happening. I stand abruptly, causing the chair to fall over. I don't even bother picking it up, I have somewhere I need to go. I just hope I'm not too late.

———

First place I stop is her work. It's on the way to her house, this way I don't by chance miss her. I hope like hell she has to work today and is inside that bar.

I yank open the door hard, causing Bo and the customers he's with to stop and look at me. I glance around and don't see any sign of Ashton. My heart sinks. I go to the bar and wait on Bo to ask him when she works again.

He comes up a few minutes later and claps me on the shoulder. "I saw you leave with Ash, all good?"

I groan, "Yes, no, well, it was until Claire. Fuck!" I rake my hands through my hair. I'm so damn pissed.

He takes a step back when I snap. "Uh oh, what happened with crazy?"

"She fucking showed up at the Honeysuckle Drive house."

"Damn… wait, you took Ashton there? Please tell me ya didn't."

Laying my head on the table, I mumble, "Yeah… I did." I know, shitty of me.

"Man, Clay." He says nothing else. He doesn't need too. I fucked up but I wasn't ready to bring her to my house. We aren't at that point. I had to be sure, plus I don't even know what this is between us. What started as an idea to fuck her out of my system sure ain't turning out so well.

I pull out the napkin and show Bo. I wait while he reads it over. He lets out a whistle while shaking his head at me.

"You know she's not wrong." He points to the napkin. "Fuck pad, that is, that's all that house is." He laughs as he pushes the napkin back toward me. I hate that he's right.

"When does she work again?"

"Actually she's due back soon. I sent her to the mart for a few items."

Thank fuck, she'll be here soon and I can explain before I have to go into work tonight. I need to clear the air with her.

When the doors open, the sun shines behind her, lighting her up. She looks absolutely breathtaking. The sun hits her hair highlighting it. Could she look any more beautiful?

She looks shocked as she looks from me to the napkin in my hand. I glance at Bo and he just waves me off, telling me it's cool to steal her away for a few.

Standing, I walk over to Ashton and take the groceries from her. She says nothing and keeps her head down. I hate that. I want to be able to look into her eyes and see everything she won't tell me.

I take the bag to Bo and then go immediately back to Ashton, who is clearly uncomfortable.

"Can we talk outside for a minute?"

What I'm not expecting is for her to shake her head no. She doesn't want to hear me out.

"Please, Ashton, I want to at least explain and clear the air between us."

"I don't think that's necessary, Clay. It's okay really, you don't have to explain."

She looks up at me and I see it. She's been crying recently. Her face is blotchy. It nearly guts me.

"Ashton." I grab her hand and rub my thumb over hers like I use to do. I'm relieved when she doesn't pull away.

"It is necessary. Please." I don't usually beg people, yet here I am begging the girl who broke my heart.

"Fine," she whispers.

Thank God. I gesture toward the door and hold it open for her. The minute we walk out, she pulls away from me, putting distance between us.

It's damn hot out here and really not where I prefer to do this, however, I know if I don't do it now, I'll lose whatever chance I have of saving anything to do with us.

I go to speak but she holds up a hand stopping me.

"Clay, whatever you have to say, please just say it. No skirting around the bush."

"I wasn't planning on it. Look, it's not exactly the way it looks."

"Then what exactly is it? What was last night?"

I move closer to her. "Last night wasn't just a fuck for me. You weren't just some girl I was hooking up with. I know it may seem that way, but Ashton, reality is you have never been just some girl." Fuck. I sigh out loud. Why is this shit so hard?

I hate that she has her arms wrapped around her body as she stares down at the gravel.

"Ashton, look at me."

She slowly raises her head to look at me, and hell if I don't move fast and place my lips on hers.

I kiss her slowly. She has to feel what I feel, that spark. When she stands stock still and doesn't really kiss me back, I start to become concerned. Not a good sign. I pull back. Maybe I shouldn't have kissed her, but I couldn't resist.

"Ashton, that house might look like the place I bring girls back to-"

"Don't lie to me, Clay."

Throwing my arms up in annoyance, I reply, "Okay, fine it was. I admit it. Do you want to know why I even have that place? Ask me why?" I don't know why I feel the need to even confess this part to her.

She tilts her head. "Why?"

"Because I couldn't bear the thought of bringing another girl to the same home I had you in. You're in every room, your memory and in the fall when the windows are opened and the scent from the apples blows through, I can't fucking take it. So I bought that little house to be able to escape to when the memories of us get to be too much. Yeah, over time I've slept with others but the main reason for that house is because of you." Running my hands through my hair, I blow out a breath.

Ashton takes a step back, shaking her head.

"I am so sorry. I'm not good for you, Clay. I've destroyed you and you deserve so much more than me." She looks exhausted.

She's not wrong, she did destroy me, but last night changed everything.

"We still have some stuff to discuss, like why you left me and all that."

"I know. Look, I wanted to tell you. I just think now isn't the time. I don't want to mess things up for you and your future."

Where is she going with this talk of my future? I just wanted to apologize, and I don't know, see if we can be friends, maybe more. Though, I have a feeling after last night I'm going to want to be more than friends.

"My future? At one time you were my future. Look, I don't know what is going on in that pretty head of yours, but I want to try to get to know you again, maybe even try to know us again."

God, I sound like some love sick fool. I reach for her, but she shakes her head.

"Clay, last night happened on a whim. You made me feel special and it was everything I would have expected it to be between us. Then Claire, and…" She suddenly stops talking.

"And what?"

"Nothing, we just can't be. I left you and nothing will ever change that."

"That's not good enough, Ashton." She's infuriating and it's hot as fuck out here. I'm starting to sweat.

"I know, but I'm no longer good enough for you. Just let it go, Clay."

Dammit to hell, why does she have to be so stubborn?

"What if I don't want to?" I have to stop myself from reaching out for her, so I place my hands on my hips instead.

And that's what breaks her hard shell. One by one the tears start falling. Shit, I've never seen such anguish written on her face.

"You just have to. You're meant to be with Claire." She turns to head back into the bar.

"Why are you so hung up on Claire?!" I half shout, fully frustrated with how this conversation is going.

Ashton stops at the door and looks back over her shoulder to me. "Because I'm trash and she's not."

She walks in, officially ending the conversation. I kick the gravel. I don't get why she keeps bringing up Claire. I don't fucking want that girl. So what, she caught us doing shit. That was before. Before I got a taste of Ashton Carpenter. My Ashton. And now that I've had a taste, I'm certain I don't want to let her go.

30

Clay

It's been a week since Ashton left me standing outside Bo's. She's left me more confused than ever. As much as I tell myself I don't need her and shouldn't want her, I do. I want her in my arms and in my bed.

I've stayed away from the bar. Bo said to give her some time and Sunny said she'll come around when she is ready. I've waited a week and I'm done waiting.

I'm on shift for another few hours, but you best believe I'm going straight to her. We are going to talk this through and figure this shit out. I've all but had it.

I'm cruising out in the land when my phone rings. I pick it up. Claire. Nope. She's caused enough issues. I decline the call. She calls back right away. Can't she take a damn hint?

"What do you want, Claire?"

"Hey, baby—"

"Nope, not your baby. Did ya need something?"

"Well, I was hoping to see you. Maybe tonight?"

"That's not gonna happen, Claire. You need to stop calling me. You've caused enough problems."

"Why not? We were getting close before Ashton got her hands on ya."

I really shouldn't entertain this, but I need to set some things straight.

"See, that's where you are wrong. She didn't put anything on me. I wanted her and I went after her. You need to get the facts before running your mouth."

"But your mama said I was gonna be good for you. Don't you wanna make her happy?"

My mama said what? Since when does she talk to her?

"Wait… you talked to my mama?"

Silence. I check my phone to make sure she didn't hang up; line is still open.

"Answer me. I don't have time for games."

"Well… yeah, we talk. We go to lunch often."

What the hell? Since when and how come no one ever told me about this?

"Since when do you do things with my mama?"

"Um... for a little bit now. We got to talkin' and she thinks I'll make you very happy and that we can be good together."

"I need to go." I hang up on her and pull up my mama in my contacts. I pause when I look at the last text my mother sent me.

Trash is not good company to keep.

Trash. Suddenly it all clicks into place. Ashton told me I didn't belong with her because she was trash. I hit the steering wheel out of frustration and drive toward town. Someone has explaining to do.

———

The minute I'm off shift, I drive straight to my mother's house. She had sold me the farm house a few years ago so she could down size. Now she has a little brick house with a white picket fence around it. I pull up to the house, but don't see her car, so I give her a call.

"Clay, dear, I was just talking about you." My mother's voice comes from the other line. She sounds all cheerful. It makes me cringe; she is probably talking to Claire.

"Who are you talking to about me?"

"Claire, dear. You know, she's just the sweetest thing."

"I don't want you talkin' to her and I sure don't want you two discussing me." I grind my teeth, growing more pissed as the minutes tick on.

"Now, dear, she's such a—"

I cut her off. "No, Mother. No but nothing. You heard what I said. I want nothing to do with Claire. Stop trying to play matchmaker."

"Is this about Ashton? You know that girl was never good enough for you." Her statement strikes a chord with me and not a good one.

"Did you run into her? Did you call her trash?" I want answers now.

"I… did run into her. I don't remember exactly what was said. It's really not important."

"What. Did. You. Say?" I ask one more time, slowly saying each word. My mother and I have had a strained relationship for years. Ever since my father's accident, she's turned into someone I barely know.

"I may have said something about trash." She laughs. It's fake, I know. I can just picture her waving her hand in the air like it's no big deal.

"I have to go, but I mean it, Mother. I want nothing to do with Claire."

I end the call and head for the next place on my list.

Pulling up the drive to Lynne's brings back a lot of memories. Ashton and I would run the land. It's where I kissed her for the first time. It holds a lot of important memories for me and I hope like hell they are important to her too.

I knock on the door twice then stand back and wait.

Lynne opens the door, a smile spreading across her face as she sees me.

"Well, boy, it's about time."

"Is she here?"

"She's out back, up in the mountain. It's been a rough week for her. I'm assuming you are here to fix all that."

Lynne's never been one to beat around the bush. She has always told it like it is.

"Yes, ma'am. I think I upset her. Well, I think my mama might have too."

She tsks. "Well, ya better get to it." With that she goes back inside leaving me on the porch.

Walking around to the back, I take in the scenery. Not much has changed.

I take the path to the only place I know she'll be. The crunching of the leaves beneath my boots will give me away.

There's no sneaking up on anyone in these woods and that's okay. I want her to know I'm here.

I spot Ashton, sitting exactly where I thought she would be, in our spot. She is sitting on a flannel blanket, with her back to me. Her hair is down, blowing gently in the breeze. She speaks first, still not looking my way.

"How'd you know where to find me?"

I come to stand up behind her. "As long as you're in Nebo, I'll always know where to find you."

She glances over her shoulder and smiles a sad smile before turning away again.

"May I sit?"

"Yeah, sure."

I sit-down next to her and drink her in. The way the sun peeks through the trees, hits her face just right. She's always been her own personal sun, so radiant.

"You're beautiful, Ash." I realize it's the first time I have called her that since she came home. It slipped off my tongue easily. She turns and looks at me, and I can see the storm in her eyes that resemble the sky. She's waging a war in her head.

"Why are you here, Clay?"

"You know why I'm here. We need to talk."

She sighs and looks away.

"Do you come up here often?" I know we need to discuss other things, yet I can't help but want to know if she comes here and thinks of me.

"Yes."

That tells me all I need to know. I reach for her hand and do what I've always done. I don't know where to start really because there's so much, but I guess I'll start with my mother.

"What did my mother say to you?"

I listen as Ashton recaps the scene in Marty's and how cold

my mother was. My mother had no right to talk to her that way, or to even try to run my life. I pull Ashton in and hold her.

"I'm so sorry for how she treated you. I don't know what's gotten into her."

"It's okay, I get it. I crushed you. She doesn't want me doing that again."

I have a feeling it's more than that, but that's for another day.

She looks at me, stares at my uniform. I didn't bother changing, I was in a rush to get here. Something passes across her face, I can't quite figure out what.

"So tell me… why did you leave me?" I ask.

Ashton sits up and pulls away from me. She leans over and pulls something out of her pocket.

"Remember my mama left me a letter?" She holds up what's in her hand.

"She always said we held her back, my pa and me. You already know this. Well, remember the day we were meeting up to go to Hillside for the bonfire?"

I nod. I do remember; she didn't show up and I had to go find her in the apple fields. When I found her, I knew instantly she was upset and when she assured me she was fine, I let it go. I didn't press further. In hindsight, I guess I should have.

"Well, you don't know this. I was on the steps of your house when I heard you and your parents talking." Ashton closes her eyes, as if talking about this causes her pain. Meanwhile I try to think back to that day. It's been years and I can't remember what we were talking about.

"Go on, what were we talking about?"

"Me," She takes a deep breath. "Your mama wanted you to go away to the police academy and said I was gonna do nothing but hold you back."

I squeeze my eyes closed. I can remember briefly. I

remember fighting with my mother over her. My mind was made up though. I had chosen Ashton. Didn't she know that?

"I think I chose you, didn't I, if I remember correctly."

"You did, but I didn't want to be that person. I didn't want to be the person holding you back. My mama left us because we held her back. Clay, I couldn't do what my mama did. I just couldn't." Her voice breaks as she squeezes my hand.

I can't believe she left me because she felt she was going to hold me back. It's such a selfless act, yet it caused us both so much heartache.

"I wish you had told me."

"I couldn't do that. I knew you would talk me out of leaving. Look at you."

She touches my chest and runs her hand down my shirt. It makes me want nothing more than to touch her, to make her feel good. My dick twitches at the thought and I try to remind myself to focus.

"You went and did it, Clay, and I can't tell you how proud I am. Me leavin' was for you to do this." Ashton pats my chest and smiles a sincere smile. She truly is proud of me.

She still thinks it was the right thing to do. I'm not sure about that.

"Why do you have your mama's letter?"

"I read it from time to time, to remind myself that I did the right thing for you."

"Can I read it?" I want to know exactly what it says. I want to understand why Ashton ran so far from me and our life.

Ashton looks at the folded paper in her hand for what feels like forever, when in reality it was only seconds before handing it to me. I carefully unfold it and begins to read it.

Ashton,

If you are reading this, then you already know
I'm gone. I just couldn't do it anymore. Your
daddy held me back and then you came
along. I tried to stay. But I wasn't happy and
I couldn't live like this anymore.
Remember this, don't let no one hold you back.
Don't hold nobody back either. It'll just end
in heartbreak. I'm sorry. I hope one day
you'll understand.
Mama

I read the note over and over as a sick feeling forms in the pit of my stomach. I study the **Y's** on the note. Each one. I close my eyes. When I open them again, I study the note all over. I think I might get sick.

"What is it, Clay? Are you okay?"

I shake my head; nothing is okay. I came for answers and now have more questions.

"Say something," she whispers.

Closing my eyes again, I let out a shaky breath. For the first time in my life I'm at a loss for words. When I feel Ashton lean over me, I open my eyes just as she places a gentle kiss on my lips.

"I'm sorry," she tells me. Ha, if she only knew I'm the person who really owes her an apology. Especially with what I'm about to tell her. I just pray she won't hate me.

"Ash," I turn toward her taking both of her hands, I don't know how to even explain, when I don't understand it myself.

"That's my mother's handwriting on that note."

31

Ashton

My entire world starts to spin even though I'm sitting down. His mother's handwriting?

"Wha… what do you mean your mother's handwriting? That can't be, my mama left it for me." Surely he's mistaken.

"I know and it sounds crazy."

He points to each of the letter Ys on my letter. "But this is my mother's writing. It's very distinct. It is how she's always written mine at the end of my name."

There's no way. I mean, the letter is very bold, like a signature mark, but how? Why? Everything starts spinning again. I close my eyes, hoping it'll help calm everything swimming through my mind.

"Ashton, say something."

I look to Clay; he looks worried and confusion is evident in his eyes.

"I… I don't know what to say. It doesn't make sense. Why would your mama leave a letter for me and my daddy?"

I've known the woman a long time, she's always been kind and caring. She even made us dishes of food when my mama first ran off.

"I don't know, but I promise you we'll figure it out. Together." Clay grips my hands a little tighter, as if I'm his lifeline just as much as he is mine.

The thought that we are in this together makes me feel a little better; however, his mama was not very happy to see me and told me to stay away from him. Just thinking of how she may react has me not wanting to figure this out.

"Clay, your mama isn't going to want to see me. She made that clear."

He looks at me a moment before leaning in to whisper in my ear.

"I don't care if my mother wants to see you or not. She's not the one I enjoy kissing."

"You enjoy kissing me?"

Clay places a kiss right below my ear, giving me goosebumps. Then another along my jawline, followed by another until he comes to my lips.

When his lips finally land on mine, they are soft and gentle. Clay takes his time kissing me slowly. I make a move to straddle him, as I grab his hair, deepening the kiss. When he grabs under my thighs to pull me closer to him, I can feel his erection straining through his cargo pants. Which, I might add, look so fucking hot on him. His entire uniform is enough to make a girl's panties wet.

I reach up under his shirt, wanting to feel his bare chest. I trace my fingers along his chiseled muscles, causing him to moan into my mouth. I love knowing I'm having this effect on him. Lord knows he has me wanting him just as bad.

In one swift move, he turns us laying me across the blanket. I hear the leaves crunching beneath it and causes me to giggle. It reminds me of our past make out sessions.

"What's so funny, Ashton?" Clay smiles down at me.

I've always been a sucker for his dimples. He could light up a room with his smile.

I smile back. "I like being with you here. I'm happy up here."

It's the truth. I could stay up here all day, just so I don't have to deal with life.

"Oh yeah?" He leans down and kisses the base of my throat.

"Mm-hmm."

Clay continues kissing me, from my collarbone to top of my breasts.

There's an unspoken need between us. I can feel it in the air. I reach for his shirt and push it up until he has no choice but to stop kissing me and lean back so I can get it off of him.

"As much as I love seeing you in uniform, I rather see you like this." I rub my hands up his torso while lightly dragging my nails back down.

Clay's back on me fast, unbuttoning my jeans. We become a tangled mess, each of us trying to get the other's clothes off, as if they can't come off fast enough.

With Clay standing above me, I take in the length of him. I don't know how I didn't pay attention during our last encounter, but he's large and thick. I dare myself to rub the bead of precum that has formed on his tip. He hisses in return.

"Ash," he whispers sternly.

I continue rubbing his tip before moving down to stroke him. He groans in pleasure and I love it. It's not long before he grabs my wrist, stilling me.

"Ash, I need to be inside you, now."

I release my hand and nod in anticipation. However, Clay doesn't make a move, he just stares at me with hooded eyes.

"Is something wrong?"

Before he goes to speak I notice the tic in his jaw.

"I don't have a condom."

"Oh, I'm honestly not worried about catching anything." If Clay's anything like the boy I use to know, he would be using protection with others.

"I'm clean. I've always used a condom with others." His voice is strained.

"Okay." And it really is.

He pulls me in and kisses me. A kiss so deep, it confirms the feelings I've been hiding for a long time. I still love him.

He guides me back down, laying me on the ground before kissing me once.

"Are you sure about this, Ashton? Out here?" Clay asks as he hovers above me.

I reach for his face. "I've never been more sure about anything in my life."

With my other hand, I reach down and take his cock and guide it between my slick folds. Clay curses under his breath as he pushes into me. The way he feels is indescribable.

"You feel so good." I hear Clay, but I'm too lost in my own pleasure to form coherent words.

And that's just what we do, we get lost in each other, out there in the woods without a worry in the world.

We headed back in after laying out there a bit. It felt freeing to just lay there with Clay, and while I have no idea what kind of hell awaits ahead, for now I'm okay.

Aunt Lynne's sitting on the porch with a glass of wine, flipping through a magazine. If I had to guess, she was waiting on us.

She looks over her magazine. "There you two are. I was beginning to wonder if y'all had gotten lost in those woods."

I try to hide my smile by biting the inside of my cheek, though I'm sure my face is beat red. Thankfully Clay comes to my rescue.

"No, ma'am, we had a lot of loss time to make up for."

No, he didn't. He might as well say we just had sex. I'm going to die of embarrassment.

"I see. Well, dinner is in the oven," she says as she goes back to reading her magazine.

"Thanks, Aunt Lynne," I say as we make our way inside to grab food.

After dishing us up some meatloaf and vegetables, we sit at the table in silence. I welcome it because it is what we both need right now. We have so much to process, I'm just glad I'm not alone.

When Clay gets up to refill our sweet teas, he finally breaks the silence.

"We need to go see my mother tomorrow."

I sigh. I don't want to, she hates me, and I don't think it'll be a pretty gathering.

"Ashton, don't close up on me. I will not allow her to speak to you the way she did at the mart."

"I know, it's just… I'm scared."

He comes up to me and sets both glasses down and begins to rub my shoulders. It's soothing and helps to ease the tension that I always seem to have.

"Listen to me." He speaks into my right ear. "No matter what happens, I'll be by your side."

I turn into him, kissing his neck. He still smells woodsy and makes me want him all over again.

"Take me home, Clay," I whisper as seductively as I can, hoping he'll pick up on what I'm hinting at.

"As long as I can have you bare again. Now that I've felt you, I don't want anything between us."

Well, shit. Alright then.

"I think I can get on board with that."

"I am going to bring you to my home, the farmhouse. It's where I should have brought you from the get go, but I wasn't sure."

"I know, I shouldn't have been so upset. I just didn't like being labeled one of your many girls."

I hate that I have caused all this. Everything that has happened is a result of me leaving.

"No, you had a right to be angry. I think we both know that you are not just another girl. You've never been just another girl."

I get up and grab him, kissing him fiercely and when we part, I know it's time to tell him how I really feel.

"I have a confession. I love you, Clay Williams. I always have and always will. I thought Brody could replace you, but the truth is I was so detached from him that I threw myself into work and enjoyed him being gone on business. It was all because I was still in love with you."

Clay's breathing has kicked up a notch. "I think it's time we got you home."

And with that we head to the farmhouse. We spend the rest of the night making up for all the lost time, cherishing and exploring each other until the sun started coming up and only then did we decide to sleep.

32

Ashton

I wake to the smell of bacon. My stomach growling reminds me that I worked up quite the appetite last night. Getting out of bed, I open Clay's closet and grab the first shirt I see, tugging it on over my head.

I pad out to where I know the smell is coming from. Standing at the stove in nothing but a pair grey joggers is the sexiest man I've ever laid eyes on. The man who owns my heart.

I quietly come up behind him and snake my arms around his waist.

"Good morning, beautiful."

"Morning, what's cookin'?"

"Eggs, bacon, and grits. There's coffee in the pot." He points to the right, I follow along spotting the coffee pot in the corner next to the sink.

I reluctantly let go of him and go over to pour some coffee.

"Did you make yourself a cup yet?"

"Not yet," he replies, winking at me.

"I'll make it."

While pouring our coffees it occurs to me how natural it is for us. It's as if we have never been apart. We flow together like tequila and salt. The thought of how good we are together makes my heart swell, even with today's impending doom.

I clean up breakfast while Clay goes out to the back patio to call his mama. He wanted to go to her house to discuss things, but I was way too uncomfortable with that option. There would be nowhere for me to run and hide while at his mama's. At least here I could lock myself in his room until she left. Clay tried to argue with me, I think mostly because he is worried about me freaking out and taking off, but in the end he agreed to have her come over here.

I'd be lying if I said I was fine. I'm actually nauseous about seeing his mother.

———

Two hours later, Mrs. Williams knocks on the door. I stay put in the living room while Clay went to answer the door.

My leg starts bouncing nervously the minute I hear her voice. It makes me want to run or vomit. Maybe both. I have to keep reminding myself to not bolt and she hasn't even stepped foot in the room yet. On instinct, I reach my hand in my pocket feeling for my mama's letter, or what might not be her letter.

"Oh, Clay dear—" Mrs. Williams shuts up the minute she notices me sitting on the couch.

She glares at me and then turns her attention back to her son.

"Clay, what is she doing here?" She looks sweetly at him. I see right through her though.

"Ashton is with me, as I told you on the phone, and there are things we need to discuss."

"I know, but I told you that I thought it would be best if we spoke in private."

Clay appears agitated as I watch their exchange.

"Again, as I told you, that was not going to happen. Now please come in and sit down." His voice is stern, like he's scolding her, and this whole scene is making me even more uncomfortable than I already am.

His mother huffs as she walks further into the living room and sits in a brown oversized chair. I take note that she sat as far away from me as she possibly could. Clay sits down next to me, instantly reaching for my hand to soothe me. I watch as his mama follows his movements. Her nose flares in disgust.

"If this is about what happened in Marty's—"

"Mother, save it. We'll get to that. First we have other matters that take priority." Clay points to a note pad and pen. I wonder when he put that there, I don't remember seeing him with it.

"Will you please write my name on this pad?"

Mrs. Williams laughs. "Why on earth do you want me to write your name?"

"I just do."

He gets up and hands her the notepad. I've never seen this side of him, though I got to give it to him, it's a genius idea. It'll either prove his claim or not. Deep down, I'm hoping he's mistaken. However, I can't get the look on his face yesterday out of my mind. He looked devastated.

The minute she uncaps the pen, I glance out the window. I can't watch. I hear Clay suck in his breath; that scares me a little. I almost want to turn and look, nope, no I don't, so I force myself to continue staring out at the trees. I wish I was out there in the orchard. I'd take the smell of rotting apples any day over sitting here right now.

"There, this is so silly. I canceled my lunch date to be here."

What a bitch. I'm sure she had plans with Claire.

"I'm sure your lunch with Claire will be missed, either way, I really don't care," Clay snaps at his mother.

I quickly turn to look at him. He sounds so angry. I look down, he's got the notepad, holding it with both hands, and they are visibly shaking.

"Clay?" I whisper, fearing what comes next.

"Give me the letter, Ashton."

The way he demands it only confirms my fears further. I slowly dig into my pocket and pull it out. He snatches right away.

"Clay, what is this silliness? I don't have time for all of this." Mrs. Williams stands as if she's gong to leave.

"Sit back down, Mother."

I'm pretty sure my mouth just hit the floor. He's never in all my years spoken to his mother in such a manner. Sure there were times that a teenage Clay was annoyed with her, but he always had respect.

His mama immediately sits back down, wiping at the imaginary wrinkles on her designer skirt.

I watch as Clay opens my letter and sets it next to the notepad. He points to the letter and looks directly at his mom. It's as if I'm not even in the room, which would be fine by me, except I am sitting here in what feels like hell.

"Were you the one who wrote the letters to Ashton and her pa, pretending to be her mother?"

Mrs. Williams rolls her eyes. "Why would I write a letter for her runaway mother? Really, this is nonsense."

The tic in Clay's jaw tells me he's pissed and growing

angrier. I want to reach out to touch him, but I'm not sure of how to calm him down.

"I'll ask you again. Did you write those letters?"

"No, Clay, I didn't. Why would I write a letter for some trashy woman who skipped town?"

No she didn't!

"Don't you talk about my mama like that!" I half shout.

"I'm only stating the facts!"

I go to tell her off, but Clay stands suddenly.

"Enough!" he shouts, startling me.

"No more bullshit. I want you," he points to his mother, "to explain why your hand writing matches the hand writing on the letter."

He said it matches. The handwriting matches. The room starts to slowly spin. Yup, I think I'm definitely going to be sick.

I barely see Clay pick up the letter and bring it over to his mama. I do, however, notice that he practically shoves it in her face. He then reaches for the notebook, holding it up.

"Why do they match?!"

I should really try to calm him down, yet I'm frozen. I can't think or focus.

Mrs. Williams's face falls as the realization hits her. She looks at me and then back to Clay.

"Why do you want to be with her? She's a runner!" Mrs. Williams all but shrieks while pointing at me.

I suck in a breath; she is brutal.

"Stop changing the subject and start explaining."

His mama looks at me again, this time holding my stare.

"You weren't meant to be with Clay. The two of you, I should have put a stop to it sooner."

"What's that supposed to mean?" I ask her.

"It means just what I said. You two weren't supposed to be

together. When Clay first brought you home, I thought it was because he had a big heart and felt sorry for you, that he pitied you, except as time went on, you two became inseparable."

"Why weren't we supposed to be together, Mother?" Clay deadpans

I stare at his mother as she closes her eyes for a moment before opening them.

"Because I was having an affair with Ashton's father.

That's the last thing I remember before everything goes black.

33

Ashton

Everything is fuzzy when I come too. I slowly sit up and try to focus.

"Easy, Ash. Just take it easy."

"What happened?"

"You passed out. Luckily, you were sitting so you didn't fall hard."

I go to nod, but everything in the room moves.

"Hey now, just lay back down." Clay's blue eyes staring back at me are full of concern.

I reach up and rub his cheek, the feel of stubble pricks at my palm.

"I'm going to ask my mother to come back in the room. Will that be okay, baby?"

Baby?

"Did you call me baby?" I'm sure I have misheard. I must have hit my head harder than Clay thinks.

"I sure did." Clay leans down and kisses me softly. I could get use to this.

"Alright, I'm gonna go bring her back in."

"K."

A few minutes pass before they both walk back into the living room. I was kind of hoping she would have left, but no such luck.

Clay comes and sits next to me, putting an arm around me. I don't bother looking at his mama. I can't.

"Mother." Clay is the first to speak.

"A long time ago, I had needs that your daddy could no longer fulfill."

Clay's daddy had been paralyzed in an accident on the farm when Clay was young. I think he was around five or six years old. He once told me that the accident had changed his mama. He didn't like to talk about that time period, and I never wanted to bring it up for fear of opening old wounds.

"Michael helped me where your daddy couldn't, if you get my drift."

"You mean screwin'! Y'all were screwin'; just come out and say it," Clay snaps. He looks so angry, and I know I should be just as angry, but too many emotions are running through me and I can't process it all.

"Okay, all right, yes, we were intimate. I had only meant for it to happen once but then we kept seeing each other. Our affair went on for a good bit until one day Beth came home early with Ashton. She had gotten sick at school."

I close my eyes and think back. I remember throwing up at school and mama coming to get me. I remember feeling awful and she had promised to make me some soup as soon as we got home. But then when we got home she became so angry. She was yelling and never did bring me soup or checked on me. I just thought she was mad at me for her having to leave work to get me. All at once the pieces start to fit together. My mama caught them.

"And what happened after y'all got caught, Mother?"

"We apologized to Beth and assured her it wouldn't happen again, except that became a lie. Michael and I couldn't stay away from each other, and I began to get greedy and jealous since I only got Michael occasionally. I couldn't stand that Beth and Ashton got him every single night."

"You had Dad," Clay grits out.

"Clay, you don't understand. Your father, while I did love him, was changed and it changed me too. I became more of his caretaker than a wife he doted on."

"What happened when you got jealous?" I ask, already not liking where it's going to go.

"I started harassing Beth."

"How very kind of you," I snap. Clay rubs my leg that is currently shaking. I know it's to calm me down, but I am thinking it's to calm himself down too at this point.

Mrs. Williams gives me a sarcastic smile.

"As I was saying, I started pestering Beth. It didn't take long before she finally started to wear down. I got desperate to get her out of the picture and did something I'm not too proud to admit, though I did it anyway. I told her I was having Michael's baby and that he was going to leave her because he loved me and our unborn baby." She sighs. "I wanted her to leave town and gave her a large amount of money to do so. I just never thought it would backfire when she left Ashton behind. That's when I snuck in and left letters, so that Michael wouldn't blame me for Beth leaving. Instead he spent the rest of his years blaming himself."

"What?!" I whisper loudly. She chased my mama off. I see red instantly and try to get my anger in check.

"What happened with the baby?" Clay asks. Oh yeah, she did say she was pregnant.

"There was never a baby. I just wanted that woman gone." She says it so matter of factly.

I'm not sure what happens next, it's almost like an out of body experience. I lunge at that despicable human who just turned my entire world upside down without a care and start pulling her hair and clawing at her face. I'm screaming, "You selfish whore!"

I continue to claw at the woman until Clay grabs at me. "Ashton! Calm down, baby."

Strong arms wrap around my waist and in the next second, I'm being pulled away from that evil woman. Waves of anger roll off me. I'm beyond livid.

"Clay, are you going to let her attack me like that?" his mother half shouts as she tries to fix her hair. Stupid bitch, it makes me want to pull her hair out all over again.

"Ashton," Clay whispers in my ear, "please."

I know he's trying to get me to calm down but there's no way. I'm too far gone at this point.

"You, you selfish bitch, I went without my mama because you had to go whore around!"

"Clay! Why are you allowing her to speak like this?!"

Is she even listening to herself? She's delusional, as if consequences don't mean jack.

"Really?!" I shout as Clay kisses the back of my head.

"Given what you have just confessed, I think she can talk to you however she wants."

Clay places kisses all along the back of my neck, and with it I feel some of the tension fade, but I'm still mad as hell. His kisses can't fix this.

Mrs. Williams huffs; she knows this is one battle she has lost.

"Did you chase Ashton off too?"

I laugh out loud at Clay's question. They both turn fast to

look at me. Hearing the words leave Clay's mouth is the tip of everything that's everything that's starting to unravel.

I watch as that terrible woman sits up straighter in her chair before speaking. "I did what I had to do." She shrugs.

What in the hell? "What's that supposed to mean?" I blurt out before Clay has a chance to ask.

"Those details aren't really important."

"Mother," Clay says in a voice I've never heard before, almost dangerous. It gives me chills.

"Only if you insist." She rolls her eyes.

"I do."

"It was one afternoon, nearing graduation. I knew Ashton would be coming over and so I might have opened up the windows to watch for her and when I saw her, I started on you about your future. I knew as long as Ashton was around, you'd never leave her. I had to intervene, especially once I found the ring in your side table drawer."

I should be surprised by the words that leave her mouth. Mrs. Williams has confessed so much in the past hour that it's sickening. This woman destroyed my family and then she destroyed the only good thing I had left. Especially after my daddy passed. Clay was all I had until that day. My entire life ruined for years! I began to thrust and fight Clay to let me go.

"Ashton!" he begs. "You could end up in jail. I know you're mad, but please, baby!"

I don't hear him though, all I focus on is everything I have lost. The countless nights I cried for my mama, Clay, my friends.

I elbow Clay hard in his stomach. I knew he wasn't expecting it by the look on his face. It shocks him and he loosens his grip. It's just enough for me to break from him. I pounce on his mother so fast, she couldn't get away, even with jumping out of her chair. I tackle her and start swinging. I punch that woman repeatedly in the face, not even caring if I black her eyes or break her nose. There's screaming and there's blood, yet I don't stop. There's so much rage built up and all at once it has come out full force.

"You're gonna pay for what you did!" I shout as I continue hitting the woman who destroyed me.

"Ashton!"

Clay somehow manages to grab my arms and pull me back off of her. She's crying and covering her face. I don't even care. I hope I mangled her pretty little face.

"I'm calling the police. She's out of control!" Mrs. Williams states as she looks up at Clay.

"Good, call them and let them know what a home wrecker you are, that you're a disgusting whore who ruined lives." I huff that last part out. Man, am I out of breath.

I watch with a smile as his mama picks up the phone and sure enough, calls for the cops. I guess you can say Clay called that one. Oh well, a trip in the back of a patrol car will be worth it.

And when the officer checks me in to do my prints and take my picture, I stand with my head held high and smile the biggest smile. This was so worth beating that woman.

34

Clay

I don't even hesitate when I jump in my truck and follow the patrol car to the station to bail Ashton out of jail. I leave my mother standing on the front porch without so much as a goodbye.

Ashton is quite the firecracker. She smiled the entire time the arriving deputy questioned and cuffed her. Deep down, I'm actually proud of her for attacking my mother. She deserved that shit. I know she's my mother and all, but she destroyed a family. She destroyed my relationship with Ashton, and all these years I spent hating *her* when it was my mother. My own mother caused Ashton to feel like she was ruining my life. Ashton had spent way to long being put down and for what?

I drive Ashton to her aunt's after she makes bail. As much as I want to hold her and comfort her, I also want her to be able to process and talk with Lynne. She's in a bit of shock over the whole thing, and I don't want to jeopardize what we may or may not have.

The other sucky part of this is that her father is no longer alive to be able to sit down and ask him about all this. He had a massive heart attack the summer she turned sixteen. There's answers she'll never get and it angers me. I, on the other hand, will be paying my mother a visit here soon.

I end up taking a personal day just to handle this shit and I never take days off. I want answers and I intend to get them.

———

Three hours later, I pull down their driveway. My father is in his wheelchair, sitting on the front porch. That's where he spends most of his days now. I wish my mother did more with him, however, I now know why. She only thinks about herself. It pisses me off and I remind myself that I need to come around more for my father. I'll take him to do stuff.

Hopping out of my truck, I catch my father's smile. I give him a small wave as I walk on up the ramp to the porch.

"Hey, Dad."

"Clay." My father nods. "How are you?"

"I've been better, truth be told." No point in sugarcoating with my old man. He's always been able to read me like an open book.

"That's understandable; try not to hate her though. She only did what she thought was best. Even if it was plain stupid."

His words take me by surprise. "You knew?"

"I knew she had a relationship with Michael Carpenter, can't really blame her for going to find intimacy that I could no longer give. I just wished she had chosen a man who was not already taken." He sighs.

"No, Dad, I don't agree with that. What happened to for better or worse? She made a vow when she married you."

I can't believe he was accepting of her behavior, I sure as hell wouldn't be. I get that he's paralyzed, but damn.

"You're right, son, but I was a broken man, never to be used again. At that point in my life, I was just glad she hadn't abandoned me."

I see his point and it must have been crushing to learn he'd never move from the waist down. He fell from a cherry picker while getting apples from the grove. He had leaned over to far to reach an apple just out of reach, stubborn man he was. It wasn't the fall itself that broke his back, it was more in the way he landed.

I remember my mom changing after the accident. She became cold and only cared about appearances. I never understood it; now I couldn't care less to try.

"Come on, boy, I suppose we should get on with it." My father's words pull me back out of my head

"Did you know that she chased Mrs. Carpenter off? And Aston?" I hope like hell he didn't. I don't want to be angry with him too.

I watch as my father closes his eyes and shakes his head. "I didn't, no, not until she told me this morning."

I nod once, holding the door open as my father wheels his way to the door. He stops and pats my hand.

"I'm sorry, Clay. I'm sorry your mother took that girl away from you. But know this: if you want that girl, you'll fight for her and you'll get her back." He turns and finishes making his way inside.

"Yes, sir," I reply, following behind him. I plan to do just that. I want my girl.

My mother is sitting on the sofa with what I'm assuming is a cup of tea in her hand. For as long as I can remember, she's always had tea in the afternoon. There's so much that's familiar, yet the woman I'm looking at has become a stranger. I don't know her, not really. Everything I thought I knew has been proven a lie.

"Hello, dear, please come in, sit down." My mother is the first to speak.

I sit in the recliner near the tv. My father has made his way to the side of the couch, next to my mother. I notice that my mother doesn't even acknowledge him and that annoys me.

I take my mother in; she looks horrendous. It's both odd and funny. I've never seen her look anything less than perfect. I'm pretty proud of my girl. She scratched her face up good and she's sporting a nice shiner that I'm sure no makeup will hide.

"How is your face?" I don't really care to know, it's just I was raised with respect and don't need my father hounding me.

"It hurts and I look absolutely terrible. I won't be able to go out in public like this." She pouts.

I just shake my head; she'll never change.

"Mother, with all due respect, you deserved that, going out in public with a black eye should be the least of your problems. You should be more concerned about what the folks around town are going to say."

No joke; there are a handful of people that already know. Everyone at the jail, Sunny, Bo, Lynne… did I mention Sunny? That girl is going to tell everyone in town, hell she'll make sure everyone all the way to Hickory knows just what a disgrace my mother is.

"Speaking of that, I'm hoping we can keep this bit of information between us. No need for everyone to know."

I laugh. "Mother, I'm sure half of Nebo already knows. You did have Ashton arrested, remember?"

"It'll be okay, Susan," my father quietly says. She turns to glare at him, as if he would never understand social status is everything to her.

"Mother," I say to steer her attention away from my father. She turns back to me.

"Do you know where Ashton's mother is or where she went when she left?" I doubt she knows or that she'll tell me, but I'm damn sure going to try, for Ashton.

"No. I gave her an envelope with cash and never saw her again." She takes a deep breath. "I'm sorry, Clay."

"You owe Ashton an apology, more so than me."

She looks down at her lap. "I know. It's just, well, aren't you at least glad she left so you could pursue your career? I mean, look at you now."

I have to grind my teeth together to keep from lashing out. Instead very calmly I say, "Yes, look at me. Do you see how angry I am with you? Do you remember how heartbroken I was? That the only girl I had ever loved and planned to spend the rest of my life with up and left without a trace? That I became a cold man. I turned into someone I didn't even know. You ruined many years of my life."

My mother can't even look at me; she keeps her head cast down. It irks me. I guess admitting fault is clearly not one of her strong suits.

Before she speaks, I watch her wipe her face, shocked because I haven't seen her cry since the day of my dad's accident.

"I'm sorry, Clay."

"I doubt you truly are. You are a terrible person for what you have done." I exhale. I need to finish up and check on Ashton. What I'm about to tell her, she won't like.

"Mother, I'm no longer giving you a cut from the farm." I hear her gasp but continue on. "When you sold me the farm, it was a done deal, clear cut. I gave you a portion monthly out of kindness. That's something you took for granted. I can think of a better way to use that money now."

When my parents sold me the farmhouse and farm, it was a done deal. I could never spend all that money so I didn't mind giving her a monthly cut. But now… now I have other plans.

I stand; my mother is full on crying now. Figures, taking away money will do that to people.

"What about your father and his medical care?" Ha, the money I gave her never went to his care. It went to her lavish shopping and her luncheons.

"Don't worry about that. I'll be handling his medical needs from here on out. That money you received each month never went to him anyway."

Her mouth falls open but no words come out. I head over to my father and lean down to hug him.

"Clay," my father quietly says, "your mama has made plenty of mistakes over the years, I won't down play 'em. However, I do hope one day you can forgive her."

I give him a hard stare. "I don't know, a lot of damage has been done and until she starts to take responsibility for her actions, nothin' will be how it was." I tip my hat to him and walk out.

Once in my truck I call Ashton, but it goes straight to voice-mail. Not gonna lie, that puts me a little on edge so I decide to drive on over to make sure everything is okay.

35

Ashton

I got on the first flight to Florida that was available. Sunny wasn't happy driving me to the airport, yet she understood. My lawyer had left me a voicemail that she could squeeze me into her schedule to sign off on my divorce. I want it over with so I can move on. Besides, with everything that has happened, I jump at the opportunity. I need some space to breathe and process.

Sunny made me promise to come home. I did, of course, considering I only packed a carry on and all my stuff is in Nebo; I kind of have to return.

My appointment is tomorrow with Glenda and thankfully she's allowing me to meet with her and will represent me in court so I don't have to go and see Brody.

For now, though, I'm enjoying my beach view from the resort that I am staying at. Listening to the waves crash over and over is soothing and good for the soul. Closing my eyes, I try to decide where to start. There's so much, it's overwhelming. I think about my mama. My mama was chased off with money and yet she didn't take me? Why? Nothing makes sense. She still left me regardless. Then there is my pa, what was he thinking? Why would he cheat on my mama? I take a sip of my mojito, just wanting to forget all of this. I'll never get answers, why dwell on it?

I met with my lawyer bright and early this morning. I'm still screwed on getting my money back from Brody. He has since filed for bankruptcy and the asshole included my investment in it. Lord, I hope I never see him again. At least it's done with. No going back. I'm looking forward, it's all I can do.

I also popped by the merchandizer I work for remotely. Well… used to work for. I decide it would be best to resign because I just can't dedicate time and I sure can't focus. So much has changed since returning home. It is for the best to leave on good terms.

Now sitting on the beach, it's refreshing to dig my toes in the sand while allowing the sun to kiss me. It's not the mountains, but comes in a close second.

As much as I'm glad to be closing this chapter of my life, there is so much uncertainty still. My future, what am I going to do? Initially, I only planned to stay in my small town just long enough to save and then get the hell out of there, except Clay stormed back into my life like a tornado. As much as my heart wants him, I'm not sure it's the right thing right now, especially with all that's been thrown at us. I'm just not sure I'm capable of loving someone or to even let someone love me.

My phone rings, bringing me out of my head. I look at the

screen, it's Sunny. I debate not answering, yet something in my gut tells me too, so I answer last minute.

"Hi, Sunny."

"Where are you?!" She sounds frantic.

"I'm on the beach currently. Why? Is everything okay?"

"Ash, there's been an accident… Clay…" Sunny trails off as I jump up off of the towel I was sitting on, dropping my phone in the process. *Clay's been in what?*

Reaching down quickly, I grab my phone; when I put it back to my ear, Sunny is shouting, "ASHTON! ARE YOU STILL THERE?!"

"Yes, yes... um..." I can't form any words.

"You need to come home, he's in the hospital!"

"Fuck! Okay. Umm. What happened? How bad is he?" My brain starts to function again and is now running a million miles a minute.

"There's no time to explain. Just let me know when you board the plane." I hear the line drop.

"Sunny, hello?" I look at my phone; sure enough, she hung up. That's not a good sign.

I take off running toward the resort, leaving my towel and water behind.

———

I am lucky enough to grab a flight exactly two hours later, with no issues. Surely that doesn't happen often. I text Sunny letting her know I was taking off and she told me she would meet outside in the drop off and pick up area.

The flight home is the longest flight of my life. I swear my knees bounce the entire time as I sit there biting my nails. I probably look like a lunatic but I don't care as I rush through the airport to meet Sunny.

I spot her jumping and waving for me. I run straight to her and instantly burst into tears. I've been able to keep my emotions in check, but now that I've touch down and about to face what lies ahead, I can't hold back.

"Is he okay?"

Sunny grabs my arms, holding me at arm's length. "He was in surgery when I left. Bo is supposed to call when he comes out." Her lips quiver slightly.

I hiccup. "How bad is he?" I'm not sure I want to know, I don't know if I can handle it.

"It was bad, Ash." She takes my bag and tosses it in the back seat. "Come on, we need to go."

I climb in the passenger seat and it hits me like a ton of bricks. Sunny is avoiding telling me any details. That means it's more than bad, like the absolute worst.

I ask no more questions as she speeds back to the hospital in Rutherford. Just knowing that's where we are going confirms how bad Clay's accident must have been.

The silence gets the best of me so I open Facebook for a distraction. Huge mistake. First thing in my newsfeed is our local news and its headline causes my breath to catch.

Ranch and grove officer in serious condition after hitting a deer.

There's two pictures, one of Clay in his uniform and the other of the wreckage. His truck is unrecognizable. I feel myself becoming nauseous and try to bite back the bile that's starting to rise. Closing out of the app, I turn my phone off. I don't want to see anything anymore. I can't take any more heartache.

Once I no longer feel like I'm going to be sick, I send up a silent prayer begging for Clay to be okay.

I stare out the window, the trees are a blur as we speed through town. I start to wonder how much heartache a person needs to go through before they fully break to the point of no return, before they die on the inside...

Shaking those thoughts, I think about the only man I love, Clay. He has to make it out of this okay. He just has too. That's just what I tell myself as we pull into the hospital. I can be dead on the inside as long as he's okay.

36

Ashton

I follow Sunny to an elevator that takes us to a smaller waiting room. It all passes by too quickly, I couldn't even tell you what floor we got off on. I spot Bo in a corner, his elbows rest on his knees, while his head is in his hands. The sight of him makes my heart drop. In the opposite corner sits Mr. And Mrs. Williams. Her face still has signs of the bruises that I put there. I'll admit I'm a little uncomfortable seeing Clay's mama. Part of me wants to go right over and slap her again. I don't of course, instead I refrain for Clay's sake. He would be upset if I caused a scene while he was fighting for his life so I focus on his father. Mr. Williams looks exhausted. It's obvious that he's upset, and I can tell he must have been crying because his eyes are bloodshot.

His parents both look up when they notice Sunny and I have arrived.

"Sunny, Ashton." Mr. Williams nods his head. His mama says nothing, just continues to fidget with the tissue in her hand.

I give a small smile in return as Sunny waves before looking at Bo.

"Bo," Sunny whispers as she goes straight to him. He stands right away and embraces her for a moment before pulling back to kiss her. Wait, what am I witnessing? Their kiss is full of passion. I have to turn away to give them some privacy. Fuck, I'm definitely going to ask Sunny what she's been keeping from me. Now's not the time though.

I find a chair as far away from Mrs. Williams as I can and plop down. I'm drained and beyond exhausted. I allow myself a few moments to close my eyes, just to try to turn off the turmoil that's all around me.

"Ashton," I hear someone call and I jump up right away.

"What?! Is he okay?! Please tell me he's okay?" I must look as crazy as I sound because Sunny comes over and starts pulling my hair back out of my face.

"Shh… yes, Clay is out of surgery. His parents are going back now with the nurse. He hasn't woken up yet," Bo says as he touches my arm.

I hate that he's not awake yet, it's killing me inside, each moment that passes and there's no update, which is strange because I'm pretty sure that part of me died somewhere along the highway. I also dislike that Clay's parents get to go back first, even though I understand that's their son and all. It still irks me as I slink back down into the seat. I try hard not to fall apart as I pull my legs up and wrap my arms around them.

When his parents come back into the waiting room, I sit up, hoping they'll have an update, that he's awake, hell, I'll take anything at this point.

"He's starting to stir. The doctor wants to give him time to wake before having anyone else back," Clay's father tells us all.

Sunny comes over and hugs me tightly.

"Soon, Ash," she whispers into my hair.

Thank heavens he is starting to wake up. I let out a breath and it eases some of the ache in my chest. I just want him to be alright.

An hour later, which was an hour of pure agony, the nurse comes back in.

"I can take one back at a time." She looks around at us.

I jump to my feet at the same time Mrs. Williams stands. Hell no, she already got to see him. She gives me a slight look of disgust. Nope, not today, bitch. I pop my eyebrow up, challenging her.

"Susan, sit down and let Ashton go on back." Mr. Williams voice is stern.

I don't wait to see her reaction, I start walking toward the nurse. I don't care what that evil woman wants right now, she's robbed me of so much. I hear her huff before finally sitting down.

"Thank fuck," I hear Bo say and it makes me smile.

The nurse smiles before turning, expecting me to follow. I hesitate and look back at Bo and Sunny, who are now wrapped in each other's arms. Sunny waves me off.

The walk is short before we turn through double doors. I hate the smell of this place. It's so sterile and not to mention bright, so bright. It's not long before we reach another set of doors. I have to wait for her to swipe her badge before we go through.

Once through, she glances at me. "Now, sweetie, Mr. Williams looks rough; please don't be alarmed though. He's had the best care and is expected to recover just fine."

Since no one else will tell me, I decide now is my only chance. "What happened to him?"

She stops and waits for me to catch up before speaking. "He hit a deer head on, looks like he might have tried to swerve just before hitting it because he ended up going off the road and rolling the truck."

"Oh my God," I whisper as my hand covers my chest.

"His face is pretty bruised up and he's got some cuts from the shattered glass. He had to have surgery to repair some internal bleeding, that is what he is just coming back from." The nurse tells me all this; however, I'm not sure I'm processing it all.

"Ma'am, are you alright, do you need to sit down?"

I vaguely feel arms come around me as the hall spins. I think I do need to sit down, but wait, what about Clay?

I shake my head. I need to get it together and stay strong. He needs me. I need him. Oh my god, I do need him, more than anything. The thought hits me so hard and clear.

"I'm fine, I'm fine. It's just a lot to take in."

"Do you want to come back later?"

"No, no… I'll be fine."

The nurse nods once, before slowly letting me go.

A few minutes later we are standing just outside his door. I suddenly become frozen, I'm not prepared to see him, not like this. I'm scared. What if he doesn't want to see me? After all, I did run off again.

The nurse gently squeezes my arm, "I didn't want to say it in front of the others, but he's been asking for ya, now go on."

"He has?" Clay's been asking for me?

"He has." The nurse shoos me toward the door. "Go, there's no need to keep him waiting." She smiles and walks off toward the nurse's station.

Taking a deep breath, I open his door and slowly walk in. I don't know where to look first. There are machines and Clay's covered in bandages and wires. He's looking like he lost an MMA fight with how bruised his face is. He is a sore sight if I ever saw one, to the point it almost knocks the wind out of me.

"Ashton," Clay calls out quietly. His voice sounds rough; it's my undoing. His deep blue eyes are trained on me, piercing me. His skin looks so pale against the stark white sheets.

All the emotions I've been fighting come out full force. I rush to him and pause just before hugging him. I have no idea where he hurts, I just know I need to touch him.

"Can I hug you?" I ask through tears.

Clay reaches for my hand and gingerly pulls me close to him. "Come here," he says as he pulls me down toward him.

Placing one hand on the pillow behind his head, I lean down and find his lips. I need to feel him, for him to feel me. I'm careful to kiss him as I don't want to pull out the tubes in his nose.

When our lips meet, I immediately feel the electricity between us. Our kiss is slow and heated. It says everything neither of us has been able to say since I returned.

I'm out of breath when I finally pull back reluctantly, not wanting him to over do it. Clay looks at me and smiles.

"I was so worried about you. I didn't know what I would do if…" I trail off.

"Stop, I'm here, it's all right. Don't go down that road." Clay rubs my hands, soothing me.

"I'm so relieved you are okay." I take in his cuts. He has several on his face, one under his left eye.

I lean and kiss his forehead and make a trail down his nose until I reach his lips again. I need this man in my life and the truth is, I'm ready to let him in.

I reluctantly pull back. I want to look him in the eyes when I say what I'm about to say.

"Clay," I swallow. I'm anxious and hope this all comes out right. "I know things haven't been the greatest between us, yet when I close my eyes all I see is you, all I feel is you."

I take a deep breath. "What I'm trying to say is that it has always been you. I love you, Clay. I never stopped, even when I tried to. It's you." I pull my bottom lip in between my teeth and wait nervously.

Clay's eyes never leave mine. "It's always been you too, Ash, and I wouldn't want anyone else by my side. Now come here and kiss me."

And I do. We kiss each other like there's no tomorrow, after all it's not promised. Clay is my second chance at love, real love, and I'm not taking it for granted this time.

Clay gently grabs my chin, causing me to look at him. "I fucking love you, Ash. Don't for one second think that I don't, you understand me?" His other hand goes behind my neck and he pulls me back in, kissing me with so much passion, I feel the fire he lights inside of me. I try to resist putting any weight on him while letting my hands carefully roam his body. I feel nothing but bandages. I worry I may be causing him pain, but I just don't want our reunion to end. However, when I see Clay wince, I pull myself back off his hospital bed.

"Hurting?" I ask. I'm afraid we might have overdone the heavy makeout session.

"A bit."

"I can go. Rest. I'll come back later."

"You'll do no such thing, Ashton. I don't want you out of my sight."

I nod once. "I'm here."

I go over and grab the guest chair and pull it up next to his bed. He instantly reaches for my hand and I give it to him. We stay like this for a while, content, just looking at the window, watching as the sun goes down.

37

Clay

I'm hurting all over this morning. I refused to let Ashton leave and watching her curl up in that small ass chair killed me, so I made her crawl in the hospital bed with me. Yeah, she tried to fight me on it at first, but in the end, I won and had the most beautiful girl in the world lying next to me. By the look on the nurses' faces, I could tell they weren't too keen about the idea, but they never said a word.

Now, looking back, it was probably a bad idea. The pain is bad and I finally asked the nurse to bring me something for the pain.

I sent Ashton down to get herself some breakfast. The cafeteria is the only place I want her going, not that I think she'll take off again. I'm just a little obsessed about my girl currently. I guess having your life flash before your eyes will do that to you.

I watch as she comes back in with coffee and a muffin. God,

she looks tired. I should send her home to shower and sleep, except I'm a selfish man.

"That's it, where is your breakfast?" I ask, winking at her.

"I'm not very hungry." She shrugs her shoulders as she sets her coffee on the side table. "Do you need anything?"

"I'm good. The nurse just came by, and they might release me tomorrow if all looks good." I sure hope everything looks good, I want to sleep in my own bed and I want Ashton under my roof.

In fact, I need to set some things straight. I'm going to clarify any doubt she might have right now.

"Don't you ever take off on me again, understand?" I keep my voice firm so she knows I'm not playing around.

Ashton's sky blue eyes look back at me in shock. She's mid bite into her muffin and I find it cute as hell.

"I wasn't running from you. I just needed to clear my head, and I also had to sign divorce papers, so it worked out," she says through chewing. I love that she is herself around me, so carefree. It's what I love about her and why I need to hear the words come out of her mouth, I need to know she's in it for real this time because I have plans, big plans.

"I wanna hear you say it, that you'll never take off on me again. Whatever you're going through, we go through together, side by side like we used to." I reach out, pulling her hand into mine. Slowly I start rubbing my thumb over her soft skin.

"Okay… I won't ever run out on you again, Clay Williams." She clicks her tongue and rolls her eyes at me in a playful manner.

My feisty woman. God, I fucking love her.

We sit in silence for a few minutes. I can barely stand it, I need to hear her voice.

"Tell me more about your dreams and career." I know she has always loved fashion. She used to bark about our little town never having a variety or style. It wasn't a surprise that when she ran off, she went into fashion.

"I, um, I'm not really sure what I want to do now. I love fashion and picking out new lines, but this town doesn't have anything like that."

A piece of her shiny blonde hair fell while she was talking, and I watch as she pulls it out of her face and moves it back behind her ear. She looks so innocent.

"What about opening up a boutique? Ever thought about something like that?" I'm hoping like hell she'll like the idea or at least think about it.

"Hmm... guess I've never thought about owning my own shop. I was just happy being the bottom man."

"Being your own boss sounds a hell of a lot better." I wink at her.

"It doesn't sound bad, but Brody screwed me out of a small chunk of money. Maybe one day I can think about opening a shop; for now it's a pipe dream."

"What do you mean Brody screwed you over?" I grow tense just thinking about the asshole.

"I saved some money over the years, and well, he needed a bit for a casino investment. I gave him the money since we were married. Looking back, it was mighty stupid of me."

"How much did ya give him, Ashton?" I practically growl at her and instantly regret it when I see her tense.

"I'm sorry, I didn't mean for it to come out like that. How much did ya give him?"

I watch Ashton as she closes her eyes and swallows hard. Shit, this can't be good.

"I'm gave him ten grand. I honestly thought he would pay me back quickly once the casino and resort were up and running. I should have pried more, paid better attention."

"Hell." I know for some that amount is no big deal, but to someone like Ashton it is. Especially given her situation.

She waves me off. "Anyhow, it is what it is and I've been able to pick up more shifts at the bar. I'll get back there one day."

That's just like her, deal and move on.

———

After one more night in the hospital, I am finally released. It feels good to breathe in the mountain air, especially after the first cool front moves on through. Bo drives Ashton and I to my house and helps me inside. The pain is still intense and I find myself dozing on and off. The last thing I remember before falling asleep on the couch in the sun room is Ashton lightly playing some nineties country.

Now slowly sitting up, I realize the sun is starting to go down. I glance around but don't see Ashton, nor do I hear any music.

"Hey, Ash?" I call out. Man, I'm stiff as a board and hurting.

When I don't get a response, I manage to stand up and wait to see what kind of pain hits. Not terrible, so I continue making my way back into the main part of the house.

"Ashton?"

Still no response. Dread fills me. Where did she go?

I make my way toward the kitchen and pause when I hear singing coming from it, her voice. The relief I felt the instant I heard her voice tells me all I need to know. She's the one.

I stand at the edge of the kitchen and just watch her. She has her back to me as she washes something in the sink. Could be dishes, could be anything, hell if I know. I take her in as she sways to "A

Little More Summertime" by Jason Aldean. Her long hair is down and tan legs go on for days. The scene in front of me takes me back. I picture a seventeen-year-old Ashton dancing on my tailgate at the bonfires. She was wild and free. He hair would tangle around her face slightly and I loved moving it away just to steal kisses. Looking at Ashton now, she really hasn't changed. She just lost herself when she left me. It's about time she gets back to living.

I continue standing there, drinking her in, until the song ends and changes to "Carolina Can" by Chase Rice. Ashton stops singing and dancing. She must not know this song, so I take it as my cue to make my presence known.

Going up behind her, I put my right hand on her hips which causes her to jump. She turns toward me, a smile on her lips. God, I love her fucking lips. I waste no time kissing her.

The minute her hands run through my hair, I feel my dick twitch. Ashton must feel it to because the next moment she grinds on me. She's being careful though, I know she is worried about me, but the more we kiss, the more I want her. I don't care how bad I'll hurt later.

"Clay," Ashton breathes along my neck and I swear it makes my dick harder.

"We can't do this, you need to heal," she says as she pulls away.

She's right, but damn. I grab her hand and pull her to me; right away she grabs my junk and smiles a devious smile.

"Well… maybe I can do a little something." She winks as she removes her hand from my erection and reaches for my hand, pulling me to the kitchen table.

"Sit," Ashton commands.

"Yes, ma'am."

I wink, liking where this may be going. Man, I hope it's going where I think it is.

Sure enough, she drags down my basketball shorts. I'm not

wearing briefs; I prefer not when I'm lounging, less restriction. My dick is now standing firmly at attention as it awaits what her next move will be.

Ashton drops down to her knees, and fuck me if it's not the sexiest thing. I lace my fingers behind my head as she takes me in her hand.

Very slowly, she takes my cock in her mouth. I hiss out. Fuck! The sensation is everything I dreamt it would be. I've thought about how her mouth would feel wrapped around me and now that it is happening, shit. I'm not sure I'll last.

As she continues to suck, her sweet mouth glides up and down my length. It feels good, too good.

"Ash… baby, I'm not gonna last if you keep this up."

"Mh-mm." Her mumbles vibrate over my dick and I nearly fucking lose it right then and there.

"Baby, you gotta stop or I'm gonna explode in your mouth." I breathe out, looking at her gorgeous face.

She looks up at me, those eyes stare back at me through her long lashes. *Fuck, Ashton, say something quick.* Ashton pauses and licks the tip of me.

"Ash," I whisper.

She says nothing, just licks her lips and smiles at me before taking me back in her mouth. Damn, her pretty little mouth is like magic. Pure magic. It doesn't take long before I feel my balls tighten.

"Fuck, Ash, just like that." I fist my hands in her hair and guide her head to keep rhythm. When she moans on my cock, I lose all control and unleash into her mouth. I watch her every move, and when she pulls back swallowing and then licking her lips, I nearly want to bend her over the damn table and take her right then and there. My body though, tells me *don't even think about it.* My body aches in pain and everything burns. Her sucking me off was worth it though, and I don't regret one bit of it. I don't care if I have to spend the rest of the day in bed.

Just when I think she can't get any more perfect, she reaches and grabs my shorts and puts them back on me; she is perfect.

"Let's get you back to bed. I can bring some food up if ya want." Ashton smiles brightly.

"Only if you come to bed too."

"I'll see what I can do." She winks as she turns toward the kitchen."Now go."

I make my way up the stairs, while thinking of ways I can convince Ashton to move in with me. Sometimes, we get another shot at mending hearts. I plan to do just that. I'm going fix us no matter what the cost will be. Ashton will be worth it and I know it's absolutely crazy, however we've lost enough time and I don't plan on losing anymore, not if I can help it.

38

Ashton

It's been a month since Clay's accident. His bruising has turned a yellowish color, barely noticeable now. He went for his follow up yesterday and the doctor is still keeping him on light duty, but he can resume most activities. He really hates it, but secretly I'm okay with that. I don't want him overdoing it, I want him to heal properly.

We have a date tonight and my shift can't end soon enough. Clay's taking me to dinner at a local place we use to go to for homecoming and prom. It's comfort food in a fancy setting. I love it and have been dreaming of country baked chicken with gravy all day.

"Girl, you got it bad," Madi calls from behind the bar.

I can't hide my smile. "Maybe I do. I don't care."

"It looks good on ya." She winks.

"Thanks."

She gets back to serving a couple of men at the bar while I

clean up a table that just left. My thoughts drift back to Clay asking me about owning a boutique. It does sound like the perfect dream job. I could bring some style to town, not to mention I would love what I'm doing. I even briefly looked up store front rentals in the nearby towns; there's just no way I could afford to open up a place right now. Between rent and then to purchase fixtures, the merchandise, and everything else, it's just not possible. I sigh. *One day, Ashton, maybe one day.*

———

By six pm I'm dressed and ready to go. I decided on a pale yellow sun dress with a denim jacket and sandals. I wrap a red bandana in my hair as a headband and knot it, leaving my hair down. I only swipe on mascara. Makeup just isn't something I have spent a lot of time on since finding myself back here. I don't have to hide who I am anymore. I give myself the once over in the mirror as I hear Aunt Lynne holler for me. Clay must be here.

"Coming!" I shout as I turn off the light and grab my wristlet.

"Well, don't you look beautiful?" my aunt says as I walk up to her.

"Thanks."

"Clay's awaiting outside for ya, I reckon you best get going."

"Yes, umm… I'm not sure if I'll be back tonight," I say shyly. I've been trying not to stay over too much, I don't want him to think I'm crowding his space.

Aunt Lynne nods once. "Go on now, don't keep him waiting."

I lean down and kiss her cheek. "Have a good night."

The drive to dinner was quiet for the most part, just the two of us playing with the radio dial until we arrived at the restaurant. We're comfortable like that, always have been.

The host brings us to a quiet booth in the corner. Perfect, because I'm still not used to prying eyes in this town. Believe it or not, people are still talking about me beating up Clay's mama.

Clay slides in next to me and we order right away. He orders country fried steak and green beans. I go with my baked chicken and gravy with a side of corn.

"How was your day?" Clay asks as he grabs my hand under the table.

"It was so slow, I'm glad work is over," I admit. "How was yours?"

"Boring until I picked you up."

"Is that so?" I playfully nudge him with my shoulder.

"Yup."

Smiling, I place a quick kiss on his cheek.

"Ashton, will ya come somewhere with me after dinner?"

His question throws me off and he sort of looks a little nervous.

"Um... sure. Where are we gonna go?"

I'm intrigued actually. It's not like him to look anything less than sure. He's always been so confident.

"You'll see, I just had to hear you agree to go." He winks and kisses me hard on my lips.

Now I'm the one who is feeling nervous. Where could he possibly want to take me and why did he have to get me to agree to go?

Our dinner arrives not long after and we casually chat in between bites of food. It is just as amazing as I remember it being years ago. Clay pays the bill the minute the server lays it on the table and drags me out of the booth as fast as he possibly can.

"Hey, hot stuff, where are ya dragging me off to in a hurry?" I ask as he pulls me out the door and down the strip plaza. "Wait, your truck is back the other way!"

Clay turns back to me while continuing to pull me along. He smirks.

"I know where my truck is. Now come on, Ash." He tugs me a little more, causing me to half run, half walk just to keep up with him.

I shake my head, laughing as I allow him to string me along.

I'm still giggling as we come to the end of the building. It breaks off allowing for two lanes of traffic to flow before another strip of building continues.

"Well, are we going to cross?" I ask Clay who has a shit eating grin on his face. "What?"

"Wouldn't this make the perfect location for your shop?"

I turn and look at the storefront. The outside is white brick with three large windows on the left side and the door is to the right of them. I walk up closer and peek through the glass door. The place is surprisingly long with wooden floors. It looks like it may have been some type of boutique in the past. There's some closet type shelving on the left side. I close my eyes briefly and picture the place painted a light gray with dark display props and tables. I think I would add light pink and maybe some gold accents to tie in. It would be beautiful.

When I open my eyes, Clay is staring, studying me.

"What's wrong?" I ask.

"Nothing. What do you think of this place?"

"It's a good size, plus it's on the corner so there's free advertisement. I could picture a clothing shop here." I point at the shop before turning back in the direction of the pickup.

"Where ya goin'?"

I turn back to Clay. "Aren't we gonna head back? I'm getting chilly."

"In a minute, come here."

I go back toward him and slightly shiver. I am still not used to the chilly evenings that North Carolina brings. Clay's still smiling like a cheeseball when he brings me into him, wrapping his arms around me.

"I can keep you warm."

"I know, I was just hoping we would head back and maybe get warm in bed." I wiggle my eyebrows, hoping he'll pick up on the hint. It's been a long few weeks of no sex and while I don't mind getting Clay off, I want to feel him inside me. I want sex.

"I want that too, baby, believe me." He breathes into my ear. "We'll get there, the night is young."

"Fine." I jokingly pout as Clay catches my bottom lip with his teeth nipping me.

"You keep this up and we won't make it to the house."

"Is that a challenge?" he mocks.

I laugh and shake my head. "Okay, why are we still here?" Seriously, we could be halfway home by now.

"Do you like it?"

I tilt my head. "Like what?"

"This place, do you think it'll make a great clothing place?"

"We're back to talkin' about this? I told you I liked it, but it's a far fetched dream. I actually looked up a few locations, there's no way I can afford anything like this, not to mention the up front costs of starting it up. Now come on, let's go." I try to tug Clay along, but he just pulls me to him and kisses my forward.

"What if I told you I purchased this place for you?"

"What?" It's barely a whisper. "I'm not sure I'm understanding."

"This building, what if I got it for you?"

I step out of Clay's arms and look at him; he is still wearing a shit eating grin.

"Clay… you didn't… tell me you didn't." God, I hope not. Anxiety starts to set in.

I watch as he reaches into his pocket and pulls something out. Slowly, he unrolls his fist and there in the palm of his hand sits a copper key. My eyes fly up to him.

"Clay is that… the key to this building?" I point to the key. I hope not.

"Yup." He walks right on up and unlocks the door.

I stand there, stunned speechless.

"Well, are you gonna come in and check it out?"

Somehow my feet move, though I'm in shock and not sure how this is even possible. Once inside, Clay flicks on a switch that lights up the entire space. It really is a fabulous set up. I look at Clay, wondering why he has done this. We've just barely gotten back together. I don't think I can accept this. It's too much. I don't want to owe anyone anything.

"Clay, did you really do this, rent this place, I mean?"

"I purchased it out right, but yes. Is everything okay, Ash?" His smile falters and I suddenly feel like a terrible person.

"But why?"

"Because you deserve it. My mother caused you a lot of devastation over the years; it's the least I could do to make up for her wrong doings."

"It ain't your job to pay for your mama's sins." I refuse to let him take the blame for the things that woman has done.

"Never said I was takin' blame. I just want to do this. I know how much you have always loved fashion. I want you to love being back home here, Ashton. I know a part of you will be lost without having a career you love."

I feel the threat of tears at his words. "I love you." I blurt the words out as my voice cracks.

"I love you too. Are you okay with this? If you are not, we can—,"

"I'm just overwhelmed, it's a lot to take in." I cut Clay off. I need him to know. I'm grateful. It's just a bit much to take in, what if I screw it up?

"Baby, I know it might seem scary, but I want you to have this. Whatever you need for it. I want to do it because I love you."

"It's gonna cost so much to get this up and running though. Clay, I can't let you do all this."

"Sure you can."

"No… what if I fail at this and it turns into a giant mistake?"

"Let's not worry about those details right now. Come check the place out, tell me what you picture."

I wipe a few tears and walk around quietly. I think about how I would set everything up. I would set up two gray counters right in the middle with a register on the counter closest to the door. I twirl around the place several times, envisioning just how I would decorate when Clay finally clears his throat.

"So, I take it you like it?"

I look over at him, his hands are shoved in his pockets as he leans against the wall.

"Like it? It's perfect! It's not gonna be easy and it's going to take so much work, but I love it!"

I run over to him and throw my arms around him, catching him off guard.

"Thank God."

Clay gently grabs my face with both hands and kisses me. It's deep, it's intoxicating. I could never get sick of the way he kisses me. He breaks the kiss way too soon leaving me hot and bothered.

"I think it's time we go home." His husky is voice telling me all I need to know.

"I couldn't agree more."

Clay laces his hand in mine and we walk out of that little boutique to head to the farmhouse.

39

Ashton

The drive back to the farmhouse is filled with sexual tension. I probably don't help the situation. I keep palming Clay, keeping him rock hard for the entire drive.

We barely make it out of the truck and into the house before we start attacking each other. Clay can't get my dress off fast enough, I'm pretty sure he may have ripped it in the process. He holds me at an arm's length and assesses me from head to toe. I'm not very comfortable being put on display like this, though my light pink bra and matching lace thong give me a little boost of confidence.

"Stop judging yourself, Ash, you look perfect. So perfect." Clay's deep voice captures my attention before he pulls me to him and starts kissing on my neck, leaving goosebumps as he makes his way to my breasts.

When he pulls my bra down, he starts sucking and nipping.

His other hand slides my thong over so he can insert a finger into me. It ignites a fire that's been waiting to be set and I don't care if it engulfs me.

"Clay... I want you inside of me now." I squirm as his fingers work their magic on me.

"Let go for me, baby, then you can have me."

He continues rubbing little circles over and over while assaulting my nipple with his tongue. The sensation quickly becomes too much as I feel myself teetering on the edge of the cliff.

"Ash, baby," Clay whispers across my chest and as the hot air from his breath hits my nipples, I fall over the edge.

"That's it, baby, just like that."

"Clay!" I hear myself scream out, but I'm too busy riding wave after wave of straight pleasure.

Clay continues kissing me all over as he starts guiding me in the opposite direction of his bedroom. I take notice, yet I can't bother to care. I'm too busy removing his shirt. I take in his fresh scars from the accident. I trace my hands over them while kissing each one. He's still gorgeous. His body is something straight out of a magazine. Sexy abs, muscled arms.

He takes us into the dining room and sets me on the table pushing place mats and the centerpiece out of the way in a rush.

"Clay, what are we doing?"

"Trust me." He winks, saying nothing as he slides the rest of his clothes off.

I watch as his cock springs free, fully erect and ready. I can't help my bite my bottom lip in anticipation. I've waited weeks for this.

Clay pulls me to the edge of the table and lines himself up at my entrance. I'm still swollen and sensitive. His touch alone sends me grinding into him, but he holds me back, resisting.

"Clay, come on, I want you now." God, I sound pathetic and whiny as I continue to try to grind into him.

"So impatient."

I grab for his cock, I'll do it myself if I have to. Clay quickly grabs my wrist though, stopping me.

"Slow down, cowgirl, and look at me."

I roll my eyes but do as he says. I look at him. His eyes are locked on mine, he's smiling and his dimples are on display. They're so sexy. I lean up and kiss each one.

"I love you, Ashton."

"I love you too."

The minute the words leave my mouth he slowly enters me. Clay thrusts slowly at first giving me time to adjust. He fills me completely before backing out and doing it all over again. It's a tease and I need him to move faster.

I start moving my hips more and it causes Clay to smirk at me.

"You want more?"

"Yes. Now."

He laughs a little, then suddenly grabs under my thighs lifting me off the table. HOLY HELL, does that feel amazing!

Clay walks us to the wall, pushing me up against it as he thrusts harder and harder.

"Oh my god!"

I claw at the back of his shoulders while he pounds into me over and over. It sends little jolts of pleasure throughout my body and I know it's only a matter of time before I lose all self control.

"I'm getting close," Clay grunts out before leaning down to bite my nipple.

He bites a little harder, causing me to yelp, but then runs his tongue over soothing where he just bit me. The pain mixed with pleasure is unlike anything I've ever felt before. It feels good, really good.

"Don't stop… Just like that!" I'm panting and out of breath, yet still want more.

I pull at his hair as I feel him lose control, both of us getting lost in each other's bliss. It's so intimate, I'm not sure I ever want to come down from this type of high.

Clay sets me down carefully after pulling out of me, resting his forehead against mine.

"Wow," is all I can say. There's no words to really describe what just happened between us. Intimacy filled with raw passion is the only way I can think to describe it.

"Wow is right." Clay's breathing is still ragged too.

I steal a quick kiss. "How sore are you?"

He laughs. "You're asking me if I'm sore, shouldn't I be asking you that?" He runs a finger between my flesh, it fires me right back up. I don't care if I'm sore, I want more.

"I'm a little sore, nothing that could stop me from another round though."

"Oh yeah? Why don't we go shower and see what else is in store for the night?"

"That sounds like the perfect plan."

Clay grabs my hand as we make our way up stairs to start the shower. I'm a little nervous, I've never showered with him. This whole situation is still new to me, what this is between us. Once in the shower, he takes his time washing me. He washes my hair and is gentle when he washes between my legs. In turn, I do the same. I lather him up and wash him slowly. We say nothing, no words are needed. This level of intimacy surpasses everything I've ever experienced.

Clay gets out of the shower first then comes back for me. He has a black towel wrapped around his waist as he dries me and then combs my hair. The gesture is enough to make me love him more than I thought I already did.

After we finished up in the bathroom, we both climbed into bed where we continued getting lost in each other for the remainder of the night.

40

Ashton

"Can you believe your grand opening is next week?" Sunny asks as she sits on the floor of my boutique folding a box of knit scarves that just arrived. They will be perfect, colder weather is on the horizon. Something that Florida didn't really take part in. Another thing to love about being back in North Carolina: there are seasons here.

"I know, I keep pinchin' myself, it doesn't seem real."

It really doesn't. Clay completely shocked me the night he unlocked the doors to this building. Since then it's been a rollercoaster ride. I refused to let him foot the entire bill. We comprised; he'll keep track of the money he fronts, and I'll pay him a portion each month once money starts rolling him. The reality is, instead of getting a loan through a bank, Clay is acting as the banker. He's given me a second chance at everything: life, love, us. I'm going to be indebted to him forever, but that's okay.

"When is Clay bringing over the display tables?"

"I think any day now. He's been busy back on the road, so he hasn't had much time." I shrug. "I'm not worried, they'll get here when they get here."

"I know, he won't let you down." Sunny laughs.

"So," I say while opening up a box of fixtures. "You and Bo, huh?" I've been so wrapped up in Clay and this place that I kept forgetting to ask her and when I did remember, we weren't alone. I also knew better to ask over text, she would just avoid it. I look at her now, and her face heats from embarrassment.

"Come on, Sunny, spill it."

"Fine, okay. Yes, we are kind of seein' each other, it ain't that big of a deal."

"Ain't that big of a deal? How so?! Of course it is."

"We don't want it to be a big deal so don't be tellin' no one. We've done just fine keeping quiet."

I laugh, they've *kind of* done a good job keeping quiet, though now when I watch them together, the signs are there. The way they've looked at each other, the whispering, I should have picked up on it sooner.

"Why keep it hidden if y'all like each other?"

"I don't know, we just don't wanna be the talk of the town and I like keepin' it between us. It keeps it fun." She gives a sly smile.

"Whatever you say, let's go grab some lunch down the way before I have to head into work."

"You just ate like an hour ago."

She's not wrong, I did, yet I feel like I'm starving.

"So? I'm still hungry."

"Alright, let's go." She gives me a questioning look, but doesn't say anything else, just jumps up off the floor and heads for the door.

————

1 week later.

It's opening day and I'm beyond nervous as I stare at myself in Clay's mirror. I'm dressed in a solid black long sleeve blouse with matching slacks and cream stilettos. I was going to pin my hair up but Clay suggested I wear I down, so I curled it a bit. I did a smoky eye look with heavy mascara. I'll admit, I haven't done myself up like this since I first came back home and it feels nice.

"You look beautiful." Clay comes to stand behind me, looking at me in the mirror.

"Why, thank you." I turn and give him a quick kiss on the cheek before turning back to give him the one over. What a sight he is too.

Clay's brown hair has been combed back; he's been blessed with nice hair. He's wearing a black and grey checkered button down with a pair of jeans. Black cowboy boots to finish him off. My oh my.

"Are you bringing your hat?" I ask even though I already know the answer.

"Yes, ma'am."

"Always the gentleman, aren't you?" I tease, stalling for a few extra minutes.

"As much as I would love nothing more than to just stay here with you, we must get goin' if we want to make it on time."

I nod. My aunt, Sunny, and Madi wanted to set up the boutique for my grand opening. They said I shouldn't be worried about setting out drinks and finger foods on my big day. My gosh, it is my big day. I'm not sure I'm ready and my stomach is a little uneasy.

"Earth to Ash."

Shit, he was talking and I was paying no attention.

"Sorry, what did you say?"

He smiles his mega smile. "Shall we?" He opens his arm for me to hook mine through before we head out.

We get there in no time, a quick twenty minute drive to town. The strip mall is bustling with people throughout. It helps me feel confident about being in this location. Clay did good.

I walk up to the front door but it is still locked. Sunny comes running over to unlock and open it for me.

"Hey!" she half shouts.

"Oh wow!" I say as I look around my boutique. There are vases with light pink roses all around the store. Their floral scent fills the air, leaving the place smelling heavenly.

There's a table with refreshments. Sweet tea and lemonade along with mini apple tarts, courtesy of Aunt Lynne. They really did go all out.

I take my time walking around, making sure everything is perfect. I brought in a nice mix from professional to trendy styles that even the locals will hopefully appreciate.

Sunny comes bouncing over. "It's time, Ash! You ready?

"Yeah, I think I am."

Sunny unlocks the doors as a few people mingle in right away. That's a good sign, I think. The commissioner comes in shortly after, carrying ribbon and a giant pair of scissors.

"Good morning, Ms. Carpenter, I'm Lori," the petite blonde says to me.

"Hey! It's so great to finally meet you! You know… to put a

face with all the emails we've exchanged," I tell her as I shake her hand.

"Likewise. Mind if I look around before starting?"

"Not at all." I wave my hand out for her to go have a look.

Clay comes up next to me, his cowboy hat firmly in place now. It should be a sin to look as good as he does.

"Are ya nervous?"

I shake my head. "Nope." I smile and lean into his ear. "Thank you for this, for making this dream my reality."

"Anything for you, Ash." He places a kiss on my cheek and then steps back. "Go on, I'll be over by Lynne." He winks and I watch as he walks off. His ass looks good in those jeans too. How did I get so lucky?

A few customers come up and ask some questions about different pieces, and two even wanted to purchase stuff, so I set them aside. I have Sunny at the counter in case people need anything right away.

About fifteen minutes later, Lori comes walking up announcing she's ready to do the ribbon cutting.

Everyone gathers just outside on the sidewalk. Clay's on one side and Sunny on the other.

"Alright, Morganton, let's give a warm welcome to Ash's Boutique! Go on, cut your ribbon." She smiles as she hands me the large scissors.

I nudge Clay. "Come on, cut it with me." I smile brightly at him. He smiles back and damn if his dimples don't have me wanting to squeeze my legs together. *Not now, Ashton.*

Together, with his hand over mine, we cut the satin red ribbon that officially puts me in business.

———

By four pm we start cleaning and shutting up the boutique. It's just the four of us: me, Clay, Sunny, and Bo. I sent Aunt Lynne home a few hours ago, and Madi went to run the bar so Bo could come toward the end. I love that it was important to Bo that he be here. It means so much to me.

"There's some apple tarts left; want one before I box them up?" Clay calls from the refreshment table.

"Sure." I finish wiping down the counter and head over to him.

I take a tart that he's holding and take a bite.

"So, ya think today went good?" I ask with a mouthful.

Clay laughs. "Good? You hit it out of the park. You should have heard what some of the women were saying about your place. They absolutely loved it, Ash." Clay beams at me and it causes my heart to swell.

"Yeah, well, I owe it all to you."

"Nah, you would have done this without me, I just gave ya a little push." He winks.

"Hey, Ash," Sunny calls from the back area. "Can you come here?"

I walk on back to her; she looks stressed.

"Is everything okay?"

"Yeah, I just started my period a little early. Happen to have anything on ya?"

"Yes, just let me grab my purse. I go back to the counter and pull out my bag and walk back toward her while opening it to pull out a tampon. When I don't find one, I start to panic. Why don't I have any on me?

"Ash," Sunny whispers, "you look like you've seen a ghost."

I slowly look up at her and then back to my bag. When is the last time I had my period?

"Ashton, hey, it's okay if ya don't have one—"

"I haven't gotten my period," I whisper, looking back to her.

"Shit, could you be…" Sunny trails off.

"No, there's no way. I'm on…" I trail off as realization hits me like a fucking Mack truck. I didn't schedule my birth control shot. I was supposed to have paperwork transferred here to a new doctor so I could make an appointment. I completely forgot with all the shit going on in my life. Oh my God. I suddenly feel like I'm going to be sick.

"Ashton, come on girl, snap out of it." Sunny looks at me with worried eyes.

"Is everything okay?" I hear Clay's voice behind me, but I silently plead for Sunny to keep her mouth shut. This. Cannot. Be. Happening.

"Just girl problems, that time of month." She laughs, playing it off.

"Oh, um... okay then…"

Once I hear his boots retreat away I let out of shaky breath.

"I'll head out and pick up a test for you, okay?" She reaches out and rubs my arm. I can only nod and fight the tears that are threatening to spill.

"How could I let this happen?"

"Shh, it'll be okay." Sunny leans in and kisses my cheek. "Ditch him and come by my place later."

"Okay."

Fuck, how am I going to get away from Clay?

41

Ashton

I hop out of Clay's truck. "I'll text ya in a bit."

"Kay, I love you, Ash."

"Love ya." I blow him a kiss and walk quickly up to Sunny's door.

I had told him that Sunny was having some relationship trouble with Bo. Yup, threw her relationship with him under the bus. It was the only thing I knew I would be able to get away with. He would have suggested we all hang out and do dinner or something, and I just couldn't have all that. I need to do this without him knowing.

Sunny opens the door, stands back, and lets me in before closing and locking it.

"How did you pull off getting away from lover boy?"

"Um... I sort of used your relationship with Bo."

"You did what?!"

"Don't kill me! I just told him you were having some trouble with Bo."

"Ugh! Ashton!"

"It's fine, you know he won't tell no one. Besides, had I not mentioned guy trouble he would have wanted to plan dinner or something with all of us. I really don't want that right now."

"That's true, I guess, but I'm still mad at you."

We stand there in her entry way for a minute; it's awkward.

"I guess I better get this over with, huh?"

"Yeah, it's in the medicine cabinet in the bathroom."

I hug her then, hard. "Thank you." I burst out crying. I haven't even taken the test yet and I'm already a mess.

Sunny pulls me back. "Look, whatever that test says in there, you will be okay."

I stand there crying, still unsure. I don't know how she can say it's going to be okay. Clay and I are barely just getting our groove back. I'm opening a business. It's too soon.

She lets me go and points to the bathroom.

I force one foot in front of the other until I reach her bathroom. I glance back at her and she gives me two thumbs up, what an asshole.

There's nothing quite like waiting for test results, a few minutes is more like an eternity, the butterflies in my stomach nearly have me sick.

The lines that start to appear change everything. Everything will be different from here on out. I stand there frozen staring at the test.

Sunny knocking on the door, startles me.

"Ash?"

I can't form words and the walls around me feel like they are starting to close in.

"What have I done?" I whisper so low I know she won't be able to hear.

More pounding. "Ashton, open up!"

I don't want to open the door; doing so will confirm that this is real. I am pregnant.

"If you don't open up, I'm calling Clay."

"No!" I shout suddenly

"Then open up this damn door!"

I hesitate for a moment before putting my hand on the lock; the second it clicks, Sunny barges in.

She looks at me and then down at the test. She grabs it off the counter, and I watch as her expression changes. Fuck. I cover my face with hands as the tears pour out.

'You're pregnant," Sunny quietly says.

I can't even acknowledge her, the tears keep coming harder and harder.

"Oh, Ashton. It's okay, this is all gonna be okay."

"I don't see how you can say that. Clay isn't going to be happy. This is all my fault." I hiccup between sobs.

"Whoa, no way. Both of y'all slept together. It's not just on you."

"I know that, but I told him all was good. It totally slipped my mind that I didn't make my next appointment. I was supposed to handle all the paperwork so the doctor could administer my shot. Every three months I am supposed to get one. Fuck!" I spit the words out so fast I think I might hyper-ventilate.

I'm so mad at myself and Clay, he's going to be so angry.

"Calm down, take a deep breath."

"I can't, this is bad, so, so bad, Sunny. Can't you see that?"

"It's not, there's worse things. Like you running off."

My eyes snap to hers. "What the hell does that mean?"

She puts her hands up in surrender.

"All I'm sayin' is I think Clay would rather deal with this," she points to the test that still in her hands, "than to deal with you leaving."

I sigh; she's probably right, yet I can't bring myself to believe her. My world is turning upside down as we speak.

"When are ya gonna tell him?"

I shake my head. "I can't think about that right now, I don't know."

"Ashton, you aren't gonna shut down. Nope. I'm calling him."

I watch as Sunny sets the test down and walks out.

"Sunny, please! Don't call him." I don't have the energy to chase after her while the contents in my stomach are still threatening to come up.

When she doesn't reply, I know she's serious, she will call him. I peek out of the bathroom and see typing on her phone. The thought of her telling him plows through my mind and the next minute I'm leaning over the toilet, upchucking the apple tarts I had earlier.

A few minutes later, Sunny comes in and is pulling my hair back, rubbing my back.

"It's gonna be okay."

"I don't know how you can say such a thing." I wipe my mouth with the back of my hand and slowly stand. I move over to the sink, washing my hands and rinsing out my mouth. The test still sits there, but I refuse to look at it again.

"Did you really call him?" I need to know.

"I called Bo and told him to bring Clay, all I said was that it was important." She gives me a weak smile.

"Oh."

"I think you should be the one to tell him, I just wanted to get him here before ya went and did something dumb, like take off."

"Gee, thanks."

"What? I'm sorry, but you freak out and take off. I can't have you leaving me again. You might not think people want you, however, we really do. You'll see."

"That's easy for you to say, Sunny, you ain't never been left behind. You don't know what it's like to not be wanted." It's a low blow, yet I use it anyway.

"Don't you use that excuse, understand?" Sunny grabs my arms forcing me to look at her.

"Clay wanted you, he's always wanted you. I wanted you, hell, even Bo wanted you. Who cares about the people who turned their back on you? They are missing out. You need to start living your life with the people who want you." Sunny pats me. "You're allowed to be happy, Ash, you deserve to be happy. Do ya understand me?" Sunny snaps at me.

I nod as I slink down to the floor, pulling my knees up to my chest. All I can think about is how Clay's going to react.

42

Clay

"Just relax, man."

Bo's words do nothing but irritate me. When he showed up, telling me we need to get to Ashton right away, my adrenaline kicked into overdrive. He said he had no idea why we had to rush to Sunny's, just that she said it was urgent. What the hell is that supposed to mean?

A million scenarios run through my mind as Bo speeds through town. Did I do something? Did I overstep with helping her get the shop up and running? Are we moving too fast? Too much too soon kind of thing? The last thing I want to do is chase her off.

"Fuck!" I shout into the cab.

"Clay, I'm sure it's nothing like what's running through that head of yours."

"Like you would know," I snap.

"Um, I do remember when Ash left you seven years ago. I was there, man, did ya forget?"

"No, I didn't fuckin' forget."

How could I? I asked a hundred questions over and over again. I spent countless hours trying to figure out why she left and if I did something wrong. Now here I am doing the same damn thing.

I called Ashton right away when I first jumped in the truck. She didn't answer so I sent a text, that too has gone unanswered. Something isn't right, and Bo is too fucking stupid to not see it.

The minute Bo pulls in the driveway, I push open the door and jump out. There's no time to wait for him to put it in park and shut the damn thing off.

I pound on the door twice with my fist. Come the fuck on and open it up.

Sunny opens the door; she looks anxious.

"Where is she?"

"She's in the bathroom."

I start to rush past her, but she stops me, grabbing me by the arm.

"Clay, Ashton is gonna need you. You understand that?" Sunny looks me in the eyes, the tone in her voice tells me it's serious. I feel my heart rate spike.

"Is everything okay?" Bo comes up behind me so I move to continue toward the bathroom. Sunny, however, keeps a tight grip on me.

"Clay, I mean it, your reaction will make or break Ash and if you break her… well, I might have to kill you."

"Sunny, what's wrong?" Bo demands, of course now he sounds nervous.

"I'll be fine as long as she's okay."

Sunny starts to let me go, but then grabs my arm again.

"She loves you."

"I know she does." I shrug off Sunny and rush down the short hall to the bathroom. Sunny's house is a small cottage style home. Two small bedrooms, one just past the bathroom and one across from it, you can see the entire house from the living room. It's that small. When I get to the bathroom, the door is shut so I knock once.

Silence. I look back at Bo and Sunny, who are still huddled near the front door. She's whispering to Bo and I don't like the look on his face.

I knock again. "Ashton, baby?"

She says nothing, but I hear the click of the lock. I turn the knob and slowly open the door. The sight of Ashton in front of me has me dropping straight to my knees.

"Baby? What's wrong?" I try to scoop her into my arms but she's rigid. I pull back. She won't even look at me.

"Ashton, talk to me."

When she still won't say anything, I nudge her chin to look at me; she's been crying hard. Her makeup is streaked down her face. It guts me to see her like this.

"Look at me," I quietly command.

I'm almost relieved when she finally does, except what I see in her eyes puts pressure back on my chest. There's so much sadness in her eyes. I lean in and put my forehead to hers.

"Talk to me, baby, please," I whisper across her lips.

"I don't want you to hate me, but will understand if ya do."

"I can't hate you, Ash. I've tried, remember? See how well that worked out?"

"This time it's different."

"What's different?"

"You can leave if ya want. If ya don't want any part of it, I'll understand."

"Baby, ya got to talk to me. I can't help if I don't know

what is wrong."

Ashton sighs heavily. "I'm pregnant, Clay." The words rush out of her mouth so fast, I think I've misheard her.

"Huh?"

"I'm pregnant," she says quietly as she bursts into tears.

She's pregnant?

"You're pregnant? Are you sure?"

"Test is on the counter."

I stand up and look down at the stick sitting on the counter; sure enough, two blue lines are visible. Well... shit. To say I'm shocked would be an understatement. Sunny's words suddenly make sense. I take a deep breath, studying the test. Our lives are about to change.

I drop back down to Ashton, and this time she allows me to pull her into my lap. I kiss her head, then her forehead, nose, and finally her lips. I wait for her to open up for me. I kiss her slowly, pouring every ounce of my heart into our kiss. I grip her neck as I continue kissing her like both of lives depend on it. It leaves us both breathless and wanting more, except right now is not the time. I wipe some of her hair back off her shoulder then stare at her stomach for a minute. There's a baby, nah scratch that, *my baby* is in there. Pride starts to swell in my chest and I know what I need to do next.

"Ashton, I love you."

She's quiet. I expect it, I've known her long enough to know when she's quiet, she's shutting down. I reach for her hand and start rubbing circles, hoping it'll bring her back around.

"Do you hear me? I love you and I ain't goin' nowhere."

I hear her sigh. That's good, she's starting to deflate. Or at least I hope she is.

"Baby, we're in this together."

"You don't hate me?" Ashton asks quietly without looking

at me.

"No, Ashton. I already told you I could never hate you. I love you, so fucking much."

"You don't have to stay just because I'm—"

"What? Don't go there. I'm right where I want to be. Sure this might be a surprise, but if there's anyone I'd want to have babies with, it's you."

Now that's the damn truth.

"I'm so sorry, Clay. I forgot all about making an appointment to continue my birth control when I moved here."

I lift her chin, causing her to look me in the eye. Her blue eyes resemble a rough sea right now. "Don't you dare apologize. We did this together. I'm just as responsible so don't go placing the blame on yourself."

There's no fucking way I'm letting her feel this way. Shit, I'm the one who didn't have a condom. Fuck.

"I guess, I just, I should have—"

"Enough, Ashton, I don't want you stuck in that head of yours."

She just nods.

"I love you."

She smiles. "I love you, Clay Williams."

"Good because you're moving in with me."

"What?!"

"Come on." I start to stand up taking her with me. I look her over. God, she's a sight, even with her makeup ruined.

"You're coming home with me. I want you in the farmhouse with me."

"No, I don't want you to move me in just because I'm…" She stops and looks down at her stomach.

I put my hand on her stomach; it causes her to tense a little.

"Because your pregnant? No, that's not the only reason I want you to move in. I have actually been planning on asking you, I just didn't want it to seem rushed. I wanted it to be the right time."

She would shit if she knew I still had the ring, the one I planned to ask her to marry me with. What's more is she would probably run for the hills if she knew I carried it with me almost daily since I got home from the hospital.

"Oh."

"So you'll move in with me?"

"I don't know, Clay, people are gonna talk. Your mama…" She trails off.

"I don't care what my mother has to say. Hell, I don't give a rat's ass what any of the folks around town say. Let 'em talk. As long as I have you at home with me, I don't care about nothin' else."

"Are you sure?"

I take both her hands in mine. "Yes. I love you and I want you to be where I am, and that's in the farmhouse."

"Okay, I'll move in, but only if—"

I cut her off with kiss to the lips. She just agreed to moving in with me. Hell yeah!

"I'm sure, now let's get out of this bathroom. Sunny has been worried."

Ashton nods her head and looks at herself in the mirror. She winces.

"Ugh, I look like hell. Can you give me a minute to clean myself up?"

"Yeah."

I pull her in and kiss her forehead before walking out, giving her some privacy.

Sunny and Bo separate themselves from each other the minute they hear me and stand up.

"Chill, I already know about you two."

"We, um… okay," Bo says as he grabs his neck. He relaxes

some and I can't help but laugh at him. It won't be long before he's in deep with her.

"Is she okay?" Sunny asks.

"She will be. It's a lot to take in."

"Yeah, but she has us."

Ashton emerges from the bathroom, carrying her heels in her hands. Her face is free of makeup and just a little blotchy from all the crying she's done. She comes up next to me, and I open my arms to pull her in. I want her close to me, but Sunny has other plans as she grabs her hands, taking her out of my hold.

"I'm so excited for y'all!" She beams.

I watch as Ashton gives a shy smile, still overwhelmed by such life altering news. We're going to be parents. My girl is going to have my baby, and I'm growing more thrilled with each minute that passes. *She's having my baby.*

"Does Bo know?" I ask Sunny.

She shakes her head, "I felt it wasn't my place to tell him."

"Ashton?" I decide to let her make the decision if she wants to tell him herself.

"You can tell him, I think I want to sit down."

Sunny and her walk over to the couch and take a seat, with Ashton leaning her head on Sunny's shoulder. For a minute, I'm slightly jealous. I should be the one comforting Ashton. I have to remind myself that she's coming home with me and I'll be able to comfort her when we are alone.

"Well, y'all gonna tell me what's goin' on?" Bo snaps me back to the forefront.

"Ashton and I are having a baby." I smile big, I don't even care how cheesy I might look. I'm so excited I want to shout from the mountain top.

"No shit?! Seriously?"

"Yup."

He comes over a claps me on the shoulder. "Congrats, man. You too, Ash."

She looks up at him and just smiles.

"Wait, you okay with this?"

I want to smack Bo for asking her that even though I know he's just as concerned as the rest of us.

"Yeah, it's just a lot to take in. I wasn't expecting this, I didn't mean for it to…" She stops talking to inhale a deep breath. I watch as she tries hard to keep her emotions in check.

I don't want her going back down that dark tunnel of what ifs so I turn the attention off of her.

"I'm fantastic and thrilled that my girl is gonna have my baby." Fuck yeah, I am.

Sunny's mouth drops into a huge smile while Bo continues his silent interrogation.

"I just knew he would be excited, Ash!" Sunny pats her knees in excitement.

"As much as I would love to stay and hang out, I'd like to get Ashton home."

"Man, you sure you are okay? What about Ashton?" Bo asks again. I know he's just worried about us, yet I find it annoying at the moment. I just want to take my girl home.

Ashton stands, going up to Bo. "I will be fine. I do want to go home and rest though. This is all overwhelming."

Bo sighs and gives her a hug and after Sunny does the same.

"Well, this was fun!" Sunny says.

It causes Ashton to smile, which in turn causes me to smile.

"Come on, baby." I walk up and snake my arm around her waist.

"I'll call ya." She waves to Sunny as we walk out.

The minute we walk out the door, we burst out laughing. Neither of us have a vehicle here. I dropped her off and then Bo picked me up to rush here. Shit.

43

Clay

After getting the keys to Bo's truck, I finally get Ashton and I out of there. The drive home is quiet. I can hear Ashton sniffling as she stares out of the window, a sign that she is silently crying. I decide to let her be and not pry. I know we have plenty to discuss.

Sunny said she would swing Bo by later to get his truck so I leave his keys under the seat and take my girl on into the house.

"Why don't you go up and run a shower? I'll make us some warm apple cider."

"You don't want to come in with me?" Ashton asks as she wipes her face.

"Do you want me to?" I had planned to give her some space, but the look on her face has me rethinking that.

"Yes, only if you want to though."

I take two long strides to get to her and wrap my hand around her neck bringing her close to my face.

"Of course I do. Don't you ever doubt that I don't want you."

I know we have a lot to work through, but I don't know how else to make her see she's everything I want. She blinks a few times, to hide the tears.

"Don't cry, Ash, let's just go shower. You'll feel a little better after."

She doesn't reply but lets me walk us up stairs to the master bath.

I start the shower, letting the water warm up first. I turn and look over at Ashton who's staring at herself in the mirror. I wonder what she sees. I wish she could see what I see in this moment. She won't though, she's always struggled with this type of stuff. I've always taken over when she couldn't handle life anymore. It makes my chest ache thinking of how she got by for the last seven years. I'm sure her jerk of an ex never comforted her. I shake my head as I make my way to stand behind her. Snaking my arms around her waist, I stare at her reflection in the mirror.

"You're so beautiful."

She gives me a small smile as I began to undress her. Once I've lifted her top over her head, I pull her hair to the side and place kisses along the back of her neck. I trace my fingers over her bra, unclasping it. When I pull the straps down her arms, her breath catches and she closes her eyes. I continue kissing her neck as I slide the black lace bra the rest of the way off.

"Unbutton your pants."

Her eyes snap open to my command just as I expected. I hold her stare with a smirk. She finally looks down as she starts to unbutton them.

I waste no time yanking them down along with her barely there panties. Stepping back to look at her, my cock instantly hardens. I start undoing my shirt as Ashton watches me in the mirror. It turns me on having her watch me undress. Her eyes follow my fingers down to the last button on my shirt. Once I slide it off, I start removing my belt. The minute Ashton bites her bottom lip, I resist the urge to take her right there on the counter. I have plans, *no need to rush this* I tell myself as I take off the rest of my clothes.

I grab her hand and pull her into the shower with me. The water stings a bit, but I welcome it as it helps to relieve some of the tension.

"I love you, Ashton."

"I love you too." She smiles at me and that alone causes my dick to twitch.

I turn her so her back is toward me and then grab my body wash but having her naked in my shower breaks down my resistance. I can't take it anymore. I have to have her.

"Place your hands on the tile."

"Huh?"

"Like this."

I take her hands, placing them in front of her on the white subway tile. God, she's so fucking sexy like this, water streaming down her back. She's leaning just slightly, enough for her ass to be on display.

"I want you, right here, right now."

Ashton turns to looks back at me, surprise evident on her face. I grab a fistful of her hair as I nudge her legs apart with mine. I place kisses along her shoulder as I position myself between her legs. She moans ever so quietly as I slowly enter her.

I try to take it easy, but it's a hard feat. I pound harder and harder each time she screams out.

With one hand on her hip, I bring my other around to her bud and start tracing circles. She's coming with me, that I'll make sure of.

"Oh God… Clay!"

"That's it, baby." I feel her start to tighten around me, so I pick up the pace.

She screams out my name again as her legs shake and her orgasm rocks her. It tips me over the edge as I thrust into her roughly. I have to wrap my arms around her waist to hold her steady.

"Holy shit," I breathe.

"Holy shit is right."

She giggles and I swear the sound of her laughter does something to my insides.

"Come on, Ash, let's get out and go to bed."

"Okay."

I take the shower head down and rinse her carefully, knowing she has to be tender. Once finished, we both climb out, dry off, and head straight for the bed where not even five minutes later, I'm making love to her all over again.

Light from the sun streaming through the window causes me to stir. It's morning and I didn't get to talk to Ashton like I had planned. We got so carried away in each other last night that nothing else mattered. I reach out for her and all I feel is a cold sheet beneath my hand. I sit up quickly and look around; she's not here. Panic sets in as I jump out of bed and grab a pair of grey joggers from my dresser.

"Ashton?" I call out. I check the bathroom on my way out, she's not in there. She can't fucking leave me, not now. No way, I won't allow it.

I take the steps two at a time as I rush down the stairs. When I don't find her in the living room, I rush into the kitchen. The French door is open, allowing a slight breeze to come through. It sends chills down my spine. She was here. I look around and a piece of paper catches my eye.

Grabbing it, I close my eyes briefly. *Please God don't let her leave me.*

You know where to find me, I'll be waiting.

"Thank fuck!" I say as I run my hand through my hair. My heart is going a mile a minute.

I think for a moment of all the places she'd be. First place that comes to mind is Lynne's, but that's a good five miles from here. There's no way she would walk that far, at least I hope not. While wracking my brain, I get the coffee going so it'll be ready and waiting once we return. As I fill the pot with water, I stare out the kitchen window. The apple trees are all picked for season, it leaves them looking bare and certainly not smelling the greatest.

I pour the pot into the machine and flick it on. It hits me. She's in the field! I take off barefoot out the door. I know exactly where she'll be: where we met all those years ago.

44

Ashton

After tossing and turning for a while, I snuck out of bed and went into the kitchen. I stare out into the fields as the sun starts to come up over the mountain side. The reality of last night comes crashing down full force. I'm pregnant with Clay's baby and he insists I move in. This is all happening too fast, it doesn't seem real. Clay still wants me after all this time and after all the heartache I've caused. There's a little voice in the back of my head telling me he's just doing this because he feels guilty about his mother's wrong doings. I push the thought away and continue looking out the window.

I start to grow more and more anxious standing there in his kitchen, wearing one of his shirts and a pair of sweats. I can barely stand it, I should go but refuse to leave him like I have in the past. Glancing around, I spot a note pad and scribble a short note. He'll know.

I open the French doors that lead out to a patio and take off.

There's a nip in the air and the ground is cool beneath my feet, however I welcome it. I need to feel something other than the turmoil in my chest.

I make it to my spot in no time and plop down between the two trees. I'm a little winded, it's been sometime since I've ran like that. Now to sit and wait, hoping the man I'm madly in love with shows.

After a few minutes, I start rethinking why I came out here. I shouldn't be alone with my thoughts, they always cause a war in my head. Coming out here used to help me clear my head. However, right now it's doing the complete opposite and I keep praying that Clay comes through the trees any minute. Like he did when we were kids.

After what felt like forever, I finally hear leaves crunching. I climb to my feet and wait.

Clay comes out through the trees. He's shirtless, wearing nothing but sweats, and hell if he doesn't look good. His chiseled abs are on display just for me.

"You came!" I can't contain myself. *Of course he came, he loves you,* I tell myself.

"You had me worried."

I instantly feel horrible for causing him worry.

I walk up to him and place my hands on his chest. Right away he wraps his arms around me, soothing me.

"I'm sorry, I didn't mean to scare you. I just needed to come out here, to ground myself."

"What can I do to help ease your mind?"

"Are you sure about me moving in with you? You don't think it's too soon?"

"Ashton, that was always the plan. Even with years lost, the plan for me hasn't changed. We might have steered in different directions for a while, but look at where we are."

I nod and take a deep breath to prevent the flood of tears

threatening to fall. Damn him for knowing how to say the right thing.

Here comes the hard question. "What about the baby?" I whisper, needing to know if he is truly on board or not, because that would change many things.

"What about the baby? Me and you, we're gonna be parents. Sure we have a lot to learn, but that's okay, we'll figure it out together."

"And you're really okay with this? I haven't ruined your life?" I don't know why I ask, I just do.

"The only thing you've ever ruined was me when you left." He unwraps from around me and takes my hand in his. "I get now why you left me and know you were only doing what you thought was right. I can't hate you for wanting me to have a better life." He pauses. "As far as the baby, I've never been so sure about anything in my life. The minute you told me you were pregnant, something changed in me and I can't quite explain it. I know for certain we are doing this together, and I can't wait to move you in so I can take care of you both."

That's Clay, always taking care of me, always wanting to help despite what I put him through.

Clay leans down, placing his lips on mine. There's something in the way that he kisses me that gives me clarity. Everything will be all right.

I pull back. "I love you, Clay, so, so much."

"I love you, baby," he breathes into my hair.

"Okay then, let's go home." I smile, looking into his deep blue eyes as I tug him back toward his house, or should I say our house?

———

Two weeks have passed since that day in the apple orchard. I didn't have much to move, got it all in one trip. Aunt Lynne seemed thrilled at the idea of Clay and I living together, but deep down, I think she was a little sad that she wasn't going to have company every night. We haven't told her about my pregnancy yet, I'm not ready to tell people, plus I wanted to wait until after my appointment to confirm everything.

I went to my first prenatal appointment today while Clay was on shift. I've decided to wait until he comes home to update him. I just hope I can hold off on calling him because I really want to tell him everything in person.

I keep busy by organizing some more of my clothes. I put a ton in the spare room closet. There's just too much.

After working on the closet, I decide to prep dinner. I'm cooking lemon chicken, rice, and steamed broccoli.

Just as I take the chicken out of the oven, I hear the door open. A smile forms on my lips immediately.

"Hey, babe."

"In the kitchen," I call out while fetching two plates from the cabinet.

"Wow, I didn't think you could get any hotter, seein' ya barefoot and pregnant in the kitchen takes you to a whole different level of hot."

I laugh and swat at him with a towel. "I'm not even showing yet!"

"So, you're still pregnant with my baby and that's hot as fuck."

"You're not so bad lookin' yourself in that uniform." I wink. "In fact I wouldn't mind watchin' you strip out of it later."

"Is that so?" he asks as he comes up and wraps a hand around the base of my neck, pulling me in for a kiss. It leaves me feeling dizzy and wanting to forget all about food. I can think of something better to do at the moment.

"So, how did your visit go?"

Dang him, guess sex will have to wait until later.

"It went really good. I got to hear the baby's heartbeat already. It was unreal!"

"What? I missed that?"

"Relax, there will be plenty of appointments. I'm only about seven weeks along. That means we can expect an early summer baby."

Clay's blue eyes twinkle in excitement as he picks me up and spins me around in a circle in the kitchen.

"Hell yeah, baby!"

"Okay, okay, put me down!" I holler through laughing.

He sets me down and drops to his knees. The movement has me sucking in a deep breath, bringing my bottom lip in between my teeth.

He lifts my shirt slightly and runs a hand over my still flat stomach.

"Daddy loves you so much already."

Oh my god, if I wasn't already pregnant, I swear my ovaries would have jumped his bones right then.

Clay then places a soft kiss on my belly before pulling my shirt down and standing back up. This man is too good for me, I swear.

"Um… we better eat before I drag ya up to the room and forget all about dinner."

"Oh no, we are going to eat first. Can't have you missing any meals now that you're growing our baby."

I huff and then wink. "Fine, but you better eat fast."

"Yes, ma'am."

THE END

EPILOGUE

Ashton
2 years later

We just celebrated our sweet baby girl, Layla Ann's second birthday. She's got her daddy's eyes and blonde hair. I'd say she is a nice mix of the two of us. I can't believe two years have flown by. It's been a wild ride full of some hiccups, but Clay and I have always come through every struggle, stronger.

I'm sitting on the front porch watching Layla scribble with sidewalk chalk on the steps. Clay's due back any time now. He had to go to the other side of the property to check on a few things at the farm; it's been a busy season.

When I see his truck coming up our long driveway I make my way to scoop Layla up. I wait for him to park before putting her back down. She squirms, fighting me to put her down, and I just laugh.

"You gotta wait, baby."

"Dada, dada!" she hollers.

As soon as Clay hops out of his truck I set her down and she takes off running for him, such a daddy's girl. I shake my head.

"Layla Ann!" he says excitedly as he squats, arms open wide for her. I keep telling myself I can't possibly fall more in love with Clay, yet every day he does something that makes me fall further.

He scoops her up and grabs stuff from the truck. I decide to go down and see if he needs a hand.

"Can I help with anything?"

"Nope," he says before handing me a bouquet of wild flowers. "These are for you."

"They're absolutely beautiful." And they are. He's picked me wild flowers for as long as I can remember. It started when we were just kids and he sorta kept doing. Now he brings me wild flowers wrapped in twine on a regular basis. I can tell ya, it never gets old.

I watch as he reaches back into the truck and pulls out a much smaller bouquet of wild flowers and hands it to Layla.

"These are for you, princess."

She beams as she takes and smells them.

"Like mama!" she shouts.

"Yup, just like mama." Clay's eyes meet mine and I can't help but smile at him.

———

After fixin' dinner and getting Layla bathed and off to bed, Clay comes down to the kitchen to help me finish up chores.

"Is she asleep?" I ask while putting dishes away.

"Yeah, she was out before I finished the book."

"I bet, she was nonstop today."

"I should be home more." Clay's words are laced with sadness.

"Nonsense, you are home plenty. It's just season right now."

The truth is, he is gone a good bit. Clay is still a ranch and grove officer full time, plus still running the apple farm. Thankfully, Blue runs the main operations and he's got a super talented bookkeeper who pays close attention to detail. I pop in occasionally with Layla, mostly on weekends. I'm just too busy during the week. Between caring for a two-year-old and running a boutique, I don't have much free time.

"I just miss you girls."

I place a kiss on his cheek. "We miss you too."

"Let's go sit out on the back patio," Clay says as he grabs the baby monitor off the counter. He's still dressed for work on the farm and while it's not his uniform, it's still equally as sexy.

"Okay, give me five and I'll meet ya out there."

I finish up in the kitchen and head out with two glasses of warm apple cider.

Sitting in the chair next to Clay, I hand him his drink. It's a little warm still, the sun has only just gone down past the mountain. A different painting graces the sky every evening and it's a sight I never get sick of seeing.

"So I've been thinking," Clay starts.

"Ha, that could be dangerous." I laugh.

"Very funny." he rolls his eyes at me and I can't help but laugh more.

"Okay, okay… you were sayin',"

"I've been thinking about our future."

"Oh yeah, what about it?"

"I'm thinkin' I want to make you my wife." Clay stands from his chair and grabs my hands bringing me to my feet.

I must have misunderstood.

"What?"

At the same time, he starts kneeling, he pulls something out of his pocket. A black velvet box. No way.

"Ashton, I've wanted to make you my wife the minute I found out you were pregnant. Hell, I had planned on purposing after graduation, but you had other plans."

"Clay," I whisper as I cover my mouth.

"I've had this ring for many years, it's the original ring I had planned on asking you to marry me with. I couldn't bring myself to get rid of it, now looking back, I'm glad I didn't."

Holy shit, I remember his mama saying he bought a ring, but there was just too much to even ask Clay about it, then I forgot all about it up until now.

"Anyhow, I thought about asking you to marry me when I found out you were pregnant. I knew. I knew then that it's you I want to spend the rest of my life with. The timing just wasn't right."

"The timing wasn't right…" I repeat him, in shock.

"I didn't want you thinking that the only reason I was marrying you was because of the baby."

I glance out at my beautiful, sleeping girl on the monitor before looking back at the black box.

"Ashton Rae Carpenter, will you marry me?" He opens the box and my eyes land on the most beautiful ring I've ever laid eyes on. Perched on the black velvet sits a lone pear shaped diamond on a white gold band. It's a classic piece, and oh so perfect.

I nod as a few stray tears fall down my cheeks.

"Yes, yes, a thousand times yes!"

Clay stands and grabs me under my ass, lifting me up. I wrap my legs around him as he spins us around.

"Yeah! I'm the luckiest man in the world!" He shouts so loud. If we had neighbors, surely they would have heard his excitement.

Clay places kisses all over my neck before lowering me and finally kissing me on the lips. His tongue is slow to enter as he places both hands on each side of my face. He caresses my checks as he deepens the kiss. It's full of passion and heat. I feel his cock straining through his jeans as he pulls me in closer. Clay has always been an amazing kisser. There's something in the way he kisses me that gets me going. It's almost too much, but not enough. He breaks the kiss too soon and right away I feel empty.

He grabs my left hand and gently puts the sparkling piece on my finger. I watch as he studies it for a moment, as if he is inspecting it.

"Woo hoo! Look at that rock!" Clay shouts.

His smile and dimples could light up the entire town of Nebo. That's how big his smile is right now. It causes me to smile back.

I place quick kiss on his lips. "Let me see!"

I hold my hand up to look at the ring, and my goodness, it takes my breath away. Clay really out did himself and to think he picked this out when he was eighteen.

"I can't believe you chose this ring when we were teens."

"I had saved up a good bit. I saw it at a jeweler in Ashville when I was with my parents getting their rings cleaned. I knew it was the one so I asked the price and started saving. It took me almost a year to save for it. I was surprised it was still available when I went back."

"Wow." I don't know what else to say. The way the moonlight hits it causes it to sparkle. I could stare at it all night.

"I love you so much, baby."

"I love you too."

I guess now is as good of a time as any to tell him my news. I pull back from him, so I can really see his face.

"So listen, babe, I have something for you too." I suck in my bottom lip.

"You do?"

"Yeah, stay right here, it's inside. I'll be right back."

I go back in and down the hall to the linen closet. I needed a hiding spot and since I knew he sure wouldn't look in there for anything, I figured it was the best spot.

I reach in and under some sheets until I find what I'm looking for. A little white box with a green and yellow ribbon on it. Taking it out, I look at it for a moment. I'm not as anxious about this little box, but still get butterflies just thinking about the anticipation of Clay's reaction.

Taking a deep breath, I take it and make my way back out to where my future husband sits.

Clay's taking a sip of his cider when I walk up to him, my hands holding the little box behind my back.

"Hey, you." I bite my bottom lip to try to contain my smile.

"I know that look. What are ya up to, Ash?"

"I'm not up to anything, I just got you a little somethin'. A little somethin' that might be a big somethin'." I laugh. It's a big something all right.

"Well, are you gonna let me have it?" His voice is husky and it nearly sends electricity throughout my body. *Will I ever grow tired of him?* Lord, I hope not.

I decide to tease him a little bit and build up the big surprise.

"How much do ya love Layla?"

He tilts his head, smiling. "As much as all the stars in the sky. Why?"

"How much do ya love me?"

"Ashton…where is this going?"

"Just answer the question, silly." I smile and wiggle my eyebrows at him.

"I love you more than anything on this earth. You're my soulmate."

I reach up and rub his cheek, while keeping the box behind my back with my other hand. I pull his lips to mine.

"I love you, Clay, so much." I pull the box from behind my back and hold it out for him.

"What's this, baby?"

"Open it."

He takes the box from me, all the while looking at me with a puzzled look. I can't wait to see his reaction; knowing him, it'll be priceless.

I watch nervously as he unties the ribbons, letting them fall to the ground. Then very carefully he opens the lid. I begin to grow more anxious with each second that passes. I start fidgeting with my fingers while waiting.

Clay pulls out a black and white image. I watch as he studies it. He's quiet, too quiet. I pull my thumb up to my mouth and start to chew on it. I'm starting to think this might not have been a good idea.

Well, shit. Confusion is etched across his face. That's not what I was going for.

"What's this, baby?"

He can't be serious, he should know what that is.

"What does it look like?" I set a hand on my hip, surely he's not clueless.

"I mean, I know what it is. Is this Layla's ultrasound picture?"

I laugh. I don't mean too, yet can't help myself.

"Ashton, what is so funny? Throw me a bone here."

"I'm sorry… sorry." I pause. "Look at it again. Look at the date."

"This was last week…" He turns and looks at me suddenly, eyes wide.

"Are you... Is this... Holy shit!" he half shouts way too loud and then looks to my stomach as I stand there grinning like a fool. This was so worth it. Seeing his reaction is everything.

I nod. "I am."

He looks back down to his hands, checking out the ultrasound picture again

"Holy shit!" He grabs me, lifting me up again. Naturally I wrap myself around him. It's as if I was molded for him and he for me. We fit perfectly.

"This is, wow! I'm so damn excited! Layla's getting a little sibling."

I lean back to look at him. "I take it you like your gift,"

"Like it? I fucking love it, baby!" Clay's dimples pop.

"Good, because there's not really a return policy on this type of gift."

Now it's Clay's turn to laugh. "Hell, no. This is a forever and ever type of gift. I can't wait!" He pauses for a minute. "When is your due date?"

"Valentine's Day."

"What?! No way!"

"Yes way."

"God, I love you, Ash."

"And I love you."

He finally sets me down and immediately drops so he's eye level with my stomach. He lifts my shirt, placing kisses while whispering I love you over and over. His gentle kisses leave chills all over me.

"Hey, baby," I lift his chin to look at me.

"Yeah?"

"I want you... like, right now."

"Out here? On the patio?"

"Yup, right now."

"Fuck, well, all right then," he growls as he stands up fast, looking at me with hooded eyes.

"Take off your clothes, Ashton."

And just like that, Clay goes all alpha on me. I'll admit, I like it when he gets like this.

Very slowly, I pull my baby blue tank top over my head, exposing my pink lace bra.

Clay starts undressing, while never taking his eyes on me. I stop for a moment to drink him in. His brown hair is a mess and his eyes are intense. His strong arms flex as he unbuttons his jeans.

"Ashton, clothes… off… now."

"Yes, Mr. Bossy." I wink as I shimmy out of my shorts and panties. No need to keep those on.

Clay's on me fast. He wastes no time lifting me and setting me on the table. Thankfully, it's not super cold beneath me.

In one swift move, Clay brings me to the edge and slides right into me. The sudden movement causes me to grab a hold of his arms while moaning in pleasure.

He pounds into me over and over as I continue to lose myself to him, it's too much.

"Clay, more." I beg.

He brings his thumb down to my clit and begins rubbing circles. Fuck.

"I feel you tightening around my cock, come on, baby, let go."

He picks up the pace and I can no longer hold on.

"Don't stop… ahh!" I scream out as I fall over the cliff and into an ocean of pleasure. He doesn't let up, not until I ride the last wave in.

Clay continues thrusting into me as I let go of his arms. I put mine behind me on the table and arch my back for him.

"Fuck, Ashton!" He reaches out to grab my breast, slightly pinching my nipple.

The pinching sends shockwaves straight down to my core and I explode all over again, except this time Clay comes along with me to ride in the wave.

We're out of breath and I can tell he's ready to collapse on top of me, but he holds his arms on either side of me as to not put weight on my stomach.

I lean up and kiss his throat that is now covered in a thin layer a sweat.

"Take me again," I whisper.

"Yes, ma'am."

And that's just what we do.

THE END

PLAYLIST

LISAMARIE CONSTANTLY LISTENS TO MUSIC FOR INSPIRATION WHILE WRITING. THIS PLAYLIST WAS CREATED & PLAYED OFTEN WHILE SHE WROTE MENDED HEARTS.

- Didn't You Know How Much I Loved You by Kellie Pickler
- That Don't Sound Like You by Lee Brice
- The End of All Things by Panic! At The Disco
- Ghost of You by 5 Seconds of Summer
- Trauma by NF
- Beautiful Crazy by Luke Combs
- Any Ol' Barstool by Jason Aldean
- Ain't Always The Cowboy by Jon Pardi
- I'm Comin' Over by Chris Young
- I Know You're Gonna Be There by Luke Bryan
- Carolina Can by Chase Rise

ACKNOWLEDGMENTS

To my readers~

Thank you for reading my books and supporting my dreams. Ya'll are the best.

Bloggers~

Thank you! If you have ever shared my books, teasers, wrote reviews, etc., know I'm so grateful for all you do. Keep blogging!

To my husband~

Thank you for the continued support. I love that I can ask your opinion and that you have no problem helping. Thank you.

To my children~

Thanks for not driving me insane while writing Mended Hearts. I love each of you so much. You are ALL my favorite!

To Erin~

Thank you for continuing to be by my side, for coming up with the title for Mended Hearts when I just couldn't decide. It's perfect and you freaking rock! Now go write your story!

To Michael~

Thank you for reading my first book while serving our country overseas. I'm so grateful for our years of friendship and all the support you have shown.

To my editor, Beth with Magnolia Author Services~

Thank you for the continued support and feedback. You have helped make Mended Hearts perfect! Thank you!

To my cover designer, Dee with Black Widow Designs~

Never in my dreams could I have pictured a more stunning cover for Mended Hearts. I couldn't be happier with how it turned out. Also, I'm slightly jealous of your creativity and talent. Thank you!

ABOUT THE AUTHOR

Lisamarie Kade is a romance author living in the sunshine state with her husband and small army of children. When not writing, she can be found chasing the kids around or volunteering for one of their many activities. Lisamarie enjoys chocolate peanut butter cups, music, and reading something steamy while sipping sweet wine.

 facebook.com/lisamariekadeauthor
 instagram.com/lisamariekadeauthor

ALSO BY LISAMARIE KADE

The Secrets We Keep

The War Within

The Christmas Breakdown